Carter dashed toward the swimming pool, took a firing stance to finish off the trucks, and was practically deafened by the sudden explosive chatter of three AK-47 automatic rifles. A searing pain ripped across the flesh of his left side.

He couldn't move a muscle without having that muscle permanently ravaged by the barrage of snarling steel being hurled his way.

The taste of failure—and of death—was sour in his throat.

It was quickly overcome by the taste of anger.

NICK CARTER IS IT!

"Nick Carter out-Bonds James Bond."
—*Buffalo Evening News*

"Nick Carter is America's #1 espionage agent."
—*Variety*

"Nick Carter is razor-sharp suspense."
—*King Features*

"Nick Carter is extraordinarily big."
—*Bestsellers*

"Nick Carter has attracted an army of addicted readers . . . the books are fast, have plenty of action and just the right degree of sex . . . Nick Carter is the American James Bond, suave, sophisticated, a killer with both the ladies and the enemy."
—*The New York Times*

FROM THE NICK CARTER
KILLMASTER SERIES

THE ALGARVE AFFAIR
ASSIGNMENT: RIO
CARIBBEAN COUP
DAY OF THE MAHDI
THE DEATH DEALER
DEATH HAND PLAY
DEATH ISLAND
THE GOLDEN BULL
THE KREMLIN KILL
THE LAST SAMURAI
THE MAYAN CONNECTION
NIGHT OF THE WARHEADS
NORWEGIAN TYPHOON
OPERATION SHARKBITE

THE PARISIAN AFFAIR
THE REDOLMO AFFAIR
REICH FOUR
RETREAT FOR DEATH
SAN JUAN INFERNO
SOLAR MENACE
THE STRONTIUM CODE
THE SUICIDE SEAT
TIME CLOCK OF DEATH
TRIPLE CROSS
TURKISH BLOODBATH
WAR FROM THE CLOUDS
THE YUKON TARGET
ZERO-HOUR STRIKE FORCE

NICK CARTER

KILLMASTER

San Juan Inferno

CHARTER BOOKS, NEW YORK

SAN JUAN INFERNO

A Charter Book/published by arrangement with
The Condé Nast Publications, Inc.

PRINTING HISTORY
Charter Original/December 1984

ISBN: 0-441-74965-8

Charter Books are published by The Berkley Publishing Group,
200 Madison Avenue, New York, New York 10016.
PRINTED IN THE UNITED STATES OF AMERICA

*Dedicated to the men of the
Secret Services of the
United States of America.*

ONE

The mountain was steeper than it had looked from the jungle floor. And higher. Nick Carter broke into a new sweat as he reached the point where the sweet, tepid aromas of the jungle gave way to the clear, piney scent of the mountain air.

He'd climbed only two thousand feet, but it had taken several thousand roundabout and strenuous paces through rugged terrain to reach that altitude.

Alto Primero was nearly four thousand feet from the valley floor. To Carter, it seemed more like four thousand *miles*.

The unaccustomed sixty-pound warpack of explosives and heavy Weatherby Mark V with scope joined with his usual weapons—the sleep Luger tucked beneath his left armpit, the slender stiletto strapped to his right forearm, and the small gas bomb taped to his groin—to take a heavy toll on his energies. His new jungle fatigues, real Green Beret issue, already looked old from sweat and the jungle's harshness.

Pausing on the mountainside, Carter shucked the fatigues and stood "invisible" in a special nightsuit. His eyes coolly scanned the walls of the villa that topped the peak in the heart of the Sierra de Luquillo Mountains,

1

fifteen miles south of San Juan, Puerto Rico. An involuntary shudder wracked his frame as he thought of having to scale that wall.

But there were miles to go before then. Calmly, doggedly, he reslung the pack and rifle, and trudged upward. Dawn was approaching. He had to strike, Hawk had said, before dawn. Or . . . Jesus, there couldn't be any "or."

David Hawk had spelled it out clearly, succinctly, during their brief meeting in his office on Dupont Circle in Washington. Was it only yesterday?

"They've built a small atomic bomb in that eagle's aerie up there in the Puerto Rican hills. We don't know precisely where they plan to set it off, but any crowded American city will serve their purpose. Destroy that bomb, Nick, and blow their laboratory to hell. After that, find the pipeline of fissionable materials that made this possible—and plug it."

The "they," of course, were Los Bravos, a group of island zealots. "They" were dedicated to the independence of Puerto Rico. Or so "they" said.

Carter knew that Los Bravos were terrorists of the first stripe, killing innocent people by droves in their fanatical drive for power. "They" would see all of Puerto Rico dead before they stopped—or were stopped.

"They" had already bombed crowded restaurants and government buildings in San Juan, and had blown up a U.S. Navy bus, killing several sailors—most of whom were Puerto Rican—and a civilian driver. "They" had sabotaged several planes at Muniz Air Force Base. "They" had a hit list that numbered in the thousands.

Following each strike, the terrorists left a machete as a token and symbol of their handiwork. They'd quickly lived up to their name: the harsh, ferocious ones.

And their actions, like their lust for power, had no conscience, no soul, no discrimination between guilty and innocent.

Atomic bombs, in the hands of such fanatics, would be very large tokens and symbols of murder that would annihilate vast numbers of the innocent and none of the guilty.

That was the way Los Bravos had chosen to fight for their cause.

Nick Carter believed in causes. He'd been embarked on one for most of his adult life, as Killmaster N3 of AXE, the ultrasecret government agency known to only a chosen few. Presumably this meant that the organization of which he was a part had two men senior to Nicholas Carter—an N1 and an N2. Not so. There had been, but both agents no longer were counted among the living on this troubled, violent planet.

And Carter's cause, bloody as it frequently was, did not subscribe to the murder of innocents.

In the case of Puerto Rico, there were peaceful ways to gain political points. The truth of the matter was that the majority of the U.S. possession's people had already spoken, had refused independent status.

Most considered themselves Americans. They wanted nothing to do with the fanatics who would destroy the island's Commonwealth status and place it under the thumb of dictatorship. And open it to wholesale exploitation.

Los Bravos listened only to their lust for power, not to the voice of the majority.

That wasn't a cause, Carter mused, flipping a drop of sweat from his strong, chiseled chin. That was an obsession, a cruel and crushing crusade that killed the innocent or made them slaves.

"We have critics," David Hawk had said during Carter's briefing in the Dupont Circle office. "Any official interference, even against the illegal building of atomic bombs, will bring a hail of criticism upon our national heads. After the Coast Guard cutter takes you as close as possible to Alto Primero, you're strictly on your own."

Carter liked being strictly on his own. But, sensibly, he'd opted for backup. If all went wrong, he could contact General Julio Pasquez at Muniz Air Force Base for simple aid and suggestions. And, if an aerial strike were needed, he had only to dial a certain number and an Air Force squadron would immediately scramble in unmarked helicopters.

"Use the second backup only in an extreme situation," Hawk had warned, his eyes softening to offset the tone of his voice. "Only *in extremis.*"

Nick Carter planned to make certain that *in extremis* didn't occur.

He'd reach the pinnacle of Alto Primero, destroy the A-bomb, and blow the laboratory to bits—and do it all on his own.

Alto Primero, loosely translated as "first highest," would no longer be a cancerous threat, no longer first highest.

The initial part of his new assignment had gone smoothly. The cutter *Griffith* had entered the mouth of the Grande de Loíza ten miles east of San Juan, had gone five miles upstream into the interior, near Carolina, and had dropped its mysterious passenger at midnight.

The drop point assured Carter a seven-mile trek across jungle floor and up mountainsides. At the end of that trek would be the bomb lab, situated in an old villa that had once been owned—and fortified—by a Spanish governor in the late nineteenth century.

Now, within sight of the south wall of the villa, Carter took his first real rest break. Using the Weatherby's infrared scope, he studied the seventy-foot-high stone wall. It would be tough getting up that wall. He checked the map Hawk had given him. There was another way in, up a narrow road that led to a gate on the north side. That road and that gate, Carter knew, would be heavily guarded. Even more important, an assault from there would give too much warning, diminishing his chances for a clean sweep.

So he'd scale the wall. If he couldn't do it with the hook and the rope, there were always the pitons and wooden mallet and braces, all tucked into the warpack with the explosives.

There were many ways to climb a wall, to seduce a lovely woman, or to skin a cat, Carter thought as he reslung the Weatherby and continued to climb. He broke into a sweat again after twenty paces. From now on, he grimly reminded himself, it would be constant movement, constant ascent, constant sweating. No time to waste.

According to Hawk's data, the finished bomb was to be moved out just past dawn and sent on its mission. Hawk didn't know where, nor did his sources. He knew only that Nick Carter had to reach the Alto Primero villa before dawn.

What Hawk had known, though, had been enough to set the veteran Killmaster's teeth on edge.

Two days ago, Hawk had said, a child on a Nassau beach had sat on what he thought was a log. The log had moved. The child had screamed.

The "log" turned out to be a man named George Pierson, a nuclear physicist who had worked at the Punta Jiguero nuclear power plant on Puerto Rico. Pierson and another physicist, Jorge Menalos, had been recruited by Los Bravos more than six months before. Pierson's story, told to a few choice ears from his hospital bed after authorities discovered who and what he was, had put a new chill into the hearts of top government officials, and had sent N3 off on this solitary jaunt into the jungles and mountains of Puerto Rico.

With the help of Pierson and Menalos, a workable laboratory had been set up at the mountaintop villa. Los Bravos had managed, through contacts yet unknown, to steal several kilograms of plutonium 239 from the Punta

Jiguero reactor on the island's northwest tip from the Punta region. Other necessary materials had been brought in from the mainland.

Pierson and Menalos had gone to work to build the bomb. It was to be a "dirty" bomb, promising maximum fallout and spread of radiation.

A month earlier, George Pierson had learned that Los Bravos planned to set off the bomb in a crowded American city, a brutal and striking warning to the U.S. government that the group meant business when they demanded independence.

At that time, Pierson had said, Jorge Menalos, a Puerto Rican by birth, was gaining influence in the heirarchy of Los Bravos. He'd become one of the leaders, with ambitious plans of his own.

But Pierson, who'd believed from the beginning that Los Bravos would merely use the bomb as leverage to gain their goals, had protested the plan to detonate the lethal weapon in a crowded city. Like Carter, he couldn't stomach the killing of innocents, no matter how worthy the cause. Not that many innocents.

A dirty bomb, dropped on Hiroshima on August 6, 1945, had instantly killed nearly eighty thousand people and maimed tens of thousands of others. Injuries and radiation sickness eventually claimed most of those. The repercussions—the illnesses—continued through the decades. And will continue.

A repeat of that catastrophe was unthinkable, Carter thought as he went on climbing. His pack seemed lighter as he thought of victory, of stopping Jorge Menalos and Los Bravos in their latest murder plan. Not even AXE had the details of that plan. George Pierson hadn't known the details. He might have learned them if he had played along.

But he hadn't. He'd let his objections be known and had stopped working on the bomb. Los Bravos had a cure for such rebellion. They put Pierson aboard a Russian freighter and paid the captain to have him killed and dumped at sea, far north of Puerto Rico.

The captain, unfamiliar with Caribbean waters, shot and dumped George Pierson just east of Nassau, where the currents carried his unconscious body to a crowded beach. A child at play saw it as a log and decided to sit on it. The log moved. The child's scream was heard, figuratively, more than a thousand miles away, in Washington, D.C.

And the story leaked out from George Pierson's hospital bed.

Common sense told the President and others that since Los Bravos had no missile system to deliver the bomb, they would most likely smuggle it stateside and trigger it in any city they chose.

The President's conjecture was backed up by military intelligence from General Julio Pasquez that, indeed, a trawler was to pick up the bomb on the southern coast of Puerto Rico and deliver it to an American port.

The possibilities were grim and limitless.

But not anymore, Carter thought as he reached the base of the villa's high wall.

With precise, measured, methodical movements, Carter released the nylon rope looped around his belly. He attached the triple-pronged hook and heaved it toward the dark heavens. It caught on the first try.

The high wall was easily breached without needing the pitons and other mountain-climbing gear. He went up the line, hand over strong hand, then gripped his fingers on the parapet and drew himself up. His tough, battle-scarred body wasn't even breathing hard. His chin on the ledge, he surveyed the shadowy compound and the dark villa beyond.

Carter's keen ears detected sound off to the left. A man walking slowly in heavy military boots. A sentry. He saw the man's shadow, then saw the shadow turn and move away.

Carter heaved himself over the wall and lay in the

shadow of the parapet. He brought up the nylon line, looped it around his waist, and replaced the hook in his belt, along with the grenades.

A motor started far in the distance, beyond the villa. A second motor started. Trucks. They were up early, the men of Los Bravos. It was still more than two hours until dawn. The villa remained dark.

Crawling in the lee of the parapet, Carter moved to his left, following the patrolling guard. He saw the trucks in front of a low garage beyond the villa, near a chain link fence. He saw the driveway and the gate. He heard voices speaking in Spanish.

Carter knew immediately what was going on, even though he couldn't hear all the words.

They were moving the bomb out early.

Why?

He had no answer for that. Only the reality of what he saw before him.

The bomb was being moved two hours early.

Pierson had said that two trucks would take the bomb to a hiding place until sometime that night. From the hiding place, the trucks would move to the southern coastal town of San Felipe where they would be picked up by the trawler.

For what destination?

Miami, perhaps. Or Washington. Or New York. Or Chicago.

Some crowded American city.

That was what George Pierson, the kidnapped and nearly dead nuclear physicist, had said.

Carter forced himself to put away those thoughts. He had to concentrate on the present, and for now, he had to stop those trucks.

He used the sniperscope on the Weatherby to check out the remainder of the compound. The guard to his left still patrolled his small area like an automaton. A half-asleep automaton.

To the right, the compound was quiet and seemingly unpopulated. There was a building beyond and to the right of the villa. A barracks, perhaps.

Near the center of the compound was a small brick building with open sides and a domed ceiling. A gazebo. Beyond it was a swimming pool. The playground of these high gods who would rule Puerto Rico.

Carter started for the gazebo and pool, crawling on his stomach, using his elbows for propulsion, holding the Weatherby in strong, calloused hands. He stopped periodically and swept the area with the sniperscope.

Red images came sharp.

The truck engines rumbled louder. Doors slammed with husky metallic clunks. Voices rose. The gate swung open on creaking, rusty hinges.

Damn. The trucks were leaving. They had to be stopped.

Carter rose from his belly, snugged the stock of the Weatherby Mark V against his shoulder, and began the long, dangerous run across the compound.

As he swung past the gazebo, he let fly with the Weatherby in single, well-aimed bursts. With a hellish roar, hunks of hot cuprosteel missiles whined across the compound.

Glass shattered. One headlight went black. A tire blew like a stick of dynamite.

Carter dashed toward the swimming pool, took a firing stance to finish off the trucks, and was practically deafened by the sudden explosive chatter of three AK-47 automatic rifles. A searing pain ripped across the flesh of his left side.

He was spun around and slammed to his belly fifty feet from the swimming pool, fifty feet past the gazebo, in a clear open space. Vulnerable space.

A frantic hand probed the wound, sending a message to his brain: plenty of blood, but not a critical hit. His dark eyes searched the blackness for the firing rifles. The knowledge he sought was quick in coming.

From three separate points—left at the top of the wall, right at the barracks, and dead ahead at a window in the dark villa—came three tongues of flame.

They had him.

He couldn't move a muscle without having that muscle permanently ravaged by the barrage of snarling steel being hurled his way.

The taste of failure—and of death—was sour in his throat.

It was quickly overcome by the taste of anger.

TWO

Calmness under fire. Perhaps the most difficult lesson any soldier can learn.

Nick Carter had learned all the lessons. Long ago.

What had Hemingway called courage? Grace under pressure? Something like that.

There was little room for grace in the ignominious position he was in, trapped on the ground by three Puerto Rican terrorists with Russian Kalashnikov AK-47 automatic rifles maintaining a withering fire.

With a flash of angry eyes, Carter again made the locations of the three flame-and-metal-flinging weapons. The firing stopped momentarily, and Carter flicked a glance at the trucks. Men were working furiously to replace the blown tire. Even as he watched, he moved forward a few feet, again using his elbows to pull himself along.

The firing started again, the bullets crashing harmlessly behind him—where he had been. The riflemen had lost him to the darkness. But why were only three men firing at him? Where were the many armed guards that manned the main gate and swarmed in the compound? Pierson had said that the guard contingent was plentiful. And why was the villa so dark? Surely, with all the shooting going on,

11

the leaders would be up, preparing to flee if things didn't
go their way.

The answers came in rapid fire, along with the whining,
crackling bullets. Most of the guards and all of the leaders
had already left the villa. The trucks conveying the nuclear bomb were the last to go. The three riflemen were all
that was left of the heavy guard contingent at this lonely
outpost.

Carter would have to remove them, pronto.

The man on Carter's left stopped firing, possibly to jam
in a new clip. Carter inched forward, timing his movement with the changing of clips, leaving a slick of his own
blood behind him.

The radical gunmen were all firing at once now, trying
to make up in quantity what they lacked in quality. Still,
one of them could get lucky. They could spot him again.
The next hit could be critical.

Carter wanted to stand up and cut loose with the Weatherby, to blast those inept gunmen to hell. But this was no
Western shoot-out, no one-on-one, face-to-face confron-
tation. While Carter would be blasting one gunman, the
other two would be pouring hot tumblers into Carter's
exposed body.

Carter swore under his breath when a familiar and
heart-sinking sound rumbled across from the main gate.
They had started the truck engines again. The tire and
headlight were fixed.

Carter moved the Weatherby out in front and hoisted it
with his hands, left hand on the stock, right on the trigger
guard. The trucks were moving, heading toward the main
gate.

A slightly quivering finger was just tightening on the
trigger when a blistering barrage of steel bracketed the
area where he lay. Cloudbursts of debris rained on him.
The *pa-pa-pa-pa-pa-pa-pow* of the AK-47s roared in his
ears.

In sensible self-defense, he flattened his hands on the

stones of the courtyard. A bullet hit the Weatherby and sent it skittering off to his right.

Even a blind pig, Nick Carter thought, recalling a phrase his father had often used, *finds an acorn once in a while.*

The trucks chugged away, unheard through the staccato, blazing rumble of the Russian weapons.

Carter was convinced that he'd miscued and had inched himself into a deathtrap. Any second now, one of those flashing, whining, whirling pellets of death would hit something vital, and that would be it.

The trucks were gone. The bomb was on its way. To some city in the U.S. To kill thousands and thousands of innocent people.

And he would die on top of this mountain.

No, dammit! No, he wouldn't die. Not yet. Not just yet. There was still time. The trucks would go into hiding until that night. Time would be needed to drive them down to San Felipe. More time would be required to smuggle the bomb aboard the trawler. And time would be required for that trawler to cross the Caribbean to an American port.

Time.

Carter needed more time. Time to stop those trucks and that trawler.

He couldn't die.

And yet he was about to.

There was one chance. A slim one. He'd planned it all along, but he hadn't expected the trucks to be repaired so soon, hadn't expected such a volley of shots at the crucial moment. He needed some old-fashioned luck now.

Courage was great. But sometimes it wasn't enough.

Carter calmed his riotous mind. He summoned inner strength. Bullets whined and spat, churning up the ancient, dank-smelling cobblestones. The hailstorm of debris continued to fall.

No luck came. He'd have to make his own.

Carter put fear from his mind and stopped thinking of

the bullets that kept blazing from those AK-47s.

Ignoring the pain in his left side, Carter rolled quickly to his right, taking advantage of a gratuitous second when it seemed that all three gunmen were changing clips. The firing started up again, and he knew he hadn't been seen. The hot, chattering steel still bracketed the area where he had been seconds before.

With effort, Carter reached inside the nightsuit and snaked Wilhelmina from her shoulder holster. He jacked a 9mm cartridge into the magazine and, using both hands to steady the familiar hunk of gleaming metal, took aim on the tongue of flame that spat out of the darkness on his left, forty yards up.

Wilhelmina boomed. The short tongue of flame that belched from her barrel was seen only by the gunman for whom the 9mm slug was intended.

There were no more bullets from that area. The gunman, Carter knew, had gone off to meet a Maker who, under the circumstances, might not be a very sympathetic listener.

Working swiftly, Carter now swung his attention to the gunman on his right, hoping to dispatch him to the same Maker before he became aware that one of his comrades had already made the trip. Wilhelmina boomed once more, its crashing noise and echo subdued by the throbbing roar of the remaining two AK-47s.

One more automatic rifle ceased to send its fiery red light into the dark morning.

There remained the man dead ahead, in a window of the dark villa. The trucks were gone now. Not even the grinding of their transmissions could be heard on the mountaintop. But it was vital that this one remaining gunman be taken alive.

Carter moved forward again, this time toward the right to circle the big swimming pool. The man in the window fired several bursts and then stopped to change a clip. In the ghostly silence, it was evident to anyone but a certified idiot that the man's fellow gunmen were no longer firing; they were either dead or out of ammunition. As if to announce his panic at guessing that bitter truth, the gunman in the window stood up and began spraying the entire courtyard with bullets.

Carter watched as bullets flew into the swimming pool, sending up geysers. He moved his eyes back to the man in the window, held Wilhelmina deathly still, and squeezed off one round.

The *ka-boom* of the Luger came at a moment when the gunman wasn't firing his rifle. The sound echoed off the villa and across the mountaintops that were now beginning to appear gray in the coming light of dawn.

Nick Carter's single bullet whined through the darkness and caught the man low in the chest, well below the heart. Carter watched as the reddened figure dropped his AK-47 and slowly tumbled out of the window. He ran to the man, praying the shot hadn't been fatal.

It had been, but not immediately. The man lay on his back, frightened eyes turned toward a lightening sky. Carter walked up swiftly, purposefully. He caught those frightened eyes with a commanding gaze. The man looked up and revealed greater fright.

"Talk!" Carter commanded.

The man shook his head. Carter could see that his fear was great and that his refusal to talk didn't spring from any deep well of courage.

"Do you speak English?" Carter demanded, keeping his eyes on the man, and keeping them hard.

The gunman, who could not have been more than seventeen years old, hesitated, then shook his head. *"No hablo ingles,"* he muttered.

"Bullshit," Carter snapped, then switched to Spanish. "You speak it and you understand it. Well, understand this, my young friend. You have a bullet in your gizzard. I have a car just down the mountainside and I can get you to a doctor. There's enough time if you talk quickly."

"What—what do you want to know, *señor*?"

"Everything you know about this place and about the atomic bomb that just left on one of those trucks."

Ten minutes later, Carter moved the bodies of all three gunmen into the empty villa. He checked the entire building and discovered all the paraphernalia necessary for the building of atomic bombs, then he began to set the explosives he'd carried up the hill in the warpack.

As the first real light touched the mountaintop, turning the black stone walls of the villa to a slate gray, Carter pressed a lever and blew the place to bits. No more bombs, of any kind, would ever be built there.

In the settled calm, with the sun glinting off his now drooping shoulders, he sat on a huge stone beside the road down from the smoldering villa, and he pondered what he had learned from the young and talkative gunman who had literally died in his arms.

The teenager's name was Santiago. He had been very helpful before he died of internal bleeding, eventually choking on his own blood. Carter had learned the names of some of the leaders. One he already knew: Jorge Menalos, the nuclear physicist who not only helped build the bomb but who aspired to top leadership. Another was Antonio Vortez, a young, hotheaded leader of a group of hardened ex-soldiers who formed the crack hit squad of Los Bravos. Another was a man known to the young gunman as Tranquilo. It was obviously a code name. Carter would have to find the man who called himself Tranquilo, just as he'd have to eliminate Antonio Vortez and reach Jorge Menalos.

Menalos was more important than either Carter or Hawk had surmised. Menalos was more than politically motivated; he was a madman of the first order.

It was bad enough, Carter thought as he sat on that stone to rest as the warming sun rose over the eastern hills, that Jorge Menalos had a second laboratory for the production of additional nuclear bombs, but there was more. There was much more, he conceded, if he could believe the words of the dying Santiago.

And Carter believed those words. Santiago hadn't known he was dying. He had spoken freely and openly because he fully believed that the man with the hard eyes and the big Luger really had a car just down the hill and would take him to a doctor, would save his life.

Carter was equally convinced that George Pierson, the nuclear physicist who had balked and had paid for his reluctance, knew nothing of the second laboratory that was on a mountaintop called, appropriately, Alto Segundo, or "second highest."

George Pierson also knew nothing of the plan to set off the first bomb in the heart of downtown San Juan.

The bomb was not to be smuggled out of Puerto Rico and set off in an American city like New York or Washington or Miami or Chicago, Carter thought, shaking his head.

No.

But it was to be set off in an American city, all right; the American city of San Juan, Puerto Rico.

Los Bravos wouldn't be the first terrorists to blow up something near and dear to them in order to gain a point, grab some publicity, achieve whatever their warped minds considered beneficial to their cause.

Even after revealing all this information, Santiago had continued to talk. "It will do you no good, *señor,* to know the location of the building where the bomb is to be taken," he had responded to Carter's direct inquiry. "Jorge Menalos is very sly. A genius. It is said that he will have the bomb rigged in such a way that the slightest interference, even the breaking in of a door at his premises, will cause it to blow up immediately. Even if you drop a conventional bomb on top of the building, the bomb will go off."

Santiago had seemed briefly proud of Menalos's genius, but he backtracked when he'd seen the grim set of

Carter's jaw and the way his knuckles turned white gripping the Luger. Carter had even thrown away a fancy cigarette with gold initials on it—and it hadn't been half smoked. Santiago's pride had diminished, and he'd seemed almost sorry for what Jorge Menalos had done.

"I am sorry, *señor*, to be the bearer of such terrible news to you," Santiago had said, choking back a gorge of blood but revealing hope of salvation in his dark brown eyes. "But there is even more."

"Tell me," Carter said, lighting up another of his custom-made cigarettes of rich Turkish blends with the NC embossed in gold on the filter. "Tell me and then we can get you to a doctor."

Santiago attempted a smile, as though he knew that it was too late for a doctor but didn't mind continuing the fiction.

"I tell you these things, *señor*," he had said, "not because of hope for life, or even fear. I tell you these things because I hope that you are a greater genius than Jorge Menalos. Perhaps you will find a way to stop him from what he is about to do. You see, I want my country to be free, to have independence, but I was born in San Juan. I love the city. I do not want it to be destroyed."

"That's understandable," Carter had said. "Will you tell me what more you have to say?"

"*Sí*. It is not much, but it is important. Time is against you, *señor*. From what I have learned from my sergeant and the others in my detachment, the bomb will be detonated at the height of the business day on Thursday. It will be set to go off at eleven o'clock."

"Jesus," Carter muttered. "And you're sure you don't know the name or location of the building?"

"I am sure, *señor*. I am as sure as . . ."

Santiago gave one final, choking, rasping wheeze and went limp in Carter's arms. Carter had propped the young guard against his knees to make it easier for him to breathe.

Now, sitting on the rock and pondering his next step, Carter checked his watch. If Santiago had spoken the truth, and if his sergeant and comrades had been fed the right data, the bomb would be detonated in about fifty-two hours.

And a big chunk of busy San Juan would be flung up in the mushroom cloud that would result.

Carter thought about Santiago's comment that the bomb was to be set off at the height of the business day. The Hiroshima bomb had been dropped just after dawn, before the business day had begun.

The thought of the potential death toll in San Juan boggled Carter's mind. It more than boggled it. It stopped all thought.

Nick Carter sat on the stone in the warm rays of the rising sun and knew that he should be rushing down the hill to start the wheels turning for a reversal of events that could lead to the death of hundreds of thousands of people, but his aching body was like his mind.

Locked.

Time was moving by. Precious minutes had already been lost. It was time to get going. With a gesture that had become automatic over the years, Carter slipped Wilhelmina into her leather nest under his arm. He rose from the stone and stretched almost lazily. And then he began to move down the mountain.

He was soon jogging. Then running.

Time, he knew, was now the most precious commodity in all of Puerto Rico.

THREE

As Nick Carter loped down the winding road toward the village of La Muda where he'd find fast transportation or know the reason why, a sense of failure haunted him. He'd failed to stop the trucks. He'd been wounded, though not badly. Of course, he had dispatched three Los Bravos soldiers and had blown up their nuclear laboratory, but a sense of anger and frustration grew within him when he faced the possibility that his failure meant that he couldn't finish this alone. He'd have to get to San Juan, then out to Muniz Air Force Base. He'd have to confer with General Julio Pasquez and accept his aid and suggestions.

In little more than forty-eight hours, a large part of downtown San Juan would be turned into an inferno. There was no time to search all the mountaintops alone, no time to look for the building containing the bomb alone, no time to trace the pipeline of fissionable materials alone.

The trouble was, Carter wanted to do it alone. He found it galling that he wouldn't be able to. Not this time, anyway.

He knew he'd have difficulty working with a team, especially a military one. But he'd accept it and adjust to its limitations. The adjustment just wasn't all that palat-

21

able, especially when Hawk had expected him to wrap this one up all by himself.

But there were other factors involved, extenuating circumstances. If he had stopped those trucks, he'd have bought enough time to have done the job himself—the whole affair. He'd have the bomb in his possession, with ample time to find the second mountaintop laboratory.

And time to find the treacherous men who were siphoning off fissionable materials from Puerto Rico's nuclear power plant and feeding them to the radical Los Bravos leaders.

Carter was sick to death of power-hungry, fanatical leaders of causes. No matter how worthy the cause, they always seemed to twist good intentions into something evil and destructive.

Puerto Rico's history was full of such men. Carter knew that history well.

Christopher Columbus was the first European to stumble across the island paradise in the Caribbean. Even with his lofty place in history, Columbus was no saint. He named the island San Juan Bautista—St. John the Baptist—and claimed it for Spain. The Arawak Indians who lived there had called the island Boriquén.

Columbus saw immense riches that he and his European masters could exploit, and spread the word back to Spain, encouraging others to come reap the harvest of his discovery.

Ponce de Leon, sent by Spain to exploit what Columbus had found, hit the jackpot when he discovered gold in abundance in the lush hills and flowing streams. In gold's honor, Ponce de Leon renamed the island Puerto Rico—Rich Port.

A succession of Spanish governors, with soldiers to kill off the Arawak Indians who protested the taking of the gold, were so good at their appointed tasks that all the gold was eventually stripped from the island.

For most of the people, rich port became poor port. But not for its leaders, however.

Through a stormy history, virtually everyone tried to get his hands on Puerto Rico. England's Sir Francis Drake put the island under siege, but the British pulled out quickly when an epidemic of plague nearly wiped out the island's population. The plague, of course, had been brought by Drake's sailors.

The French and the Dutch also tried to wrench Puerto Rico away from Spanish rule, ostensibly to stop the Spaniards from looting the country of its riches. The real reason was that they wanted to loot the island themselves.

Moves for independence began as early as the mid-nineteenth century. Progress in this direction halted when Luis Muñoz Rivera made peace with the Spanish lords and set about establishing some kind of self-rule to eliminate the poverty that Spanish rule had wrought. Unfortunately, the continuing push for independence came to a temporary end when the Spanish-American War broke out and Puerto Rico became an American possession in 1898. Following a period of American military rule, agitation for self-rule rose once again. In 1917 the U.S. Congress bowed to pressure and voted full American citizenship to Puerto Ricans.

Things quieted until the Great Depression, when economic chaos and individual poverty spawned fanatical leaders who introduced terrorism and violence into a new push for independence. But the people of Puerto Rico still felt a need for American support in a world turning ever more frequently to violence to solve its problems. After nationalist fanatics tried to assassinate President Truman in 1950, the U.S. Congress once again awoke, and in July 1952, Puerto Rico was granted Commonwealth status, with its own constitution and own governor.

Good and bad leaders followed. Good and bad factions developed and grew healthy.

Some of the people are content with the status quo—Commonwealth status with U.S. support and federal aid.

Some want full statehood. They expend quiet and well-planned efforts to set the island's affairs in order for that eventuality.

Some want total independence.

It is this volatile minority that resorts to terrorism and violence.

As Carter thought about the history of the island, and of those who believe that bloodshed and death are the only answers, he became convinced that he had the answer to the question he had asked Santiago just before the man died.

Why do the leaders want to kill so many of their own people?

The answer was quite simple.

Men like Jorge Menalos, Antonio Vortez, and the mysterious one referred to as Tranquilo, would then be able to say to the U.S. government that the people of Puerto Rico were willing to die to the last man in the drive to gain independence.

In fact, few were willing to die for such a cause. And certainly not Menalos and Vortez and Tranquilo.

Carter would bet his last nickel that when the bomb went off, that trio would be far removed from the blasting point, from ground zero. They would show up later in an attempt to pick up the pieces. Or pick to pieces what was left.

And how far were these fanatics willing to go in their lust for power and death? Carter wondered. If the U.S. didn't give in after San Juan was destroyed, would the fanatics use the bombs now being built in that second mountain lab—on Alto Segundo—to destroy other cities on the island?

Would they, like the Spaniards, pluck everything of value from the people of their island country and then install an ironclad rule over the survivors?

Carter ran faster. Precious time was running out.

Shortly after nine A.M. the telephone rang in the office of General Julio Pasquez. The general's secretary, a pretty, dark-haired Air Force sergeant, answered, then immediately buzzed the inner office. The general's aide picked up the receiver, listened a few moments, spoke a few words, listened, spoke again, listened, then spoke again.

The conversation would have meant little to anyone hearing only the aide's part. The person on the other end of the line did most of the talking.

"Just as you had warned us, Colonel Sangre, he showed up a few hours before dawn. The trucks were loaded and being prepared for departure. Most of us had already left. This madman disabled one of the trucks, but our loyal guards kept him at bay until the truck was repaired and safely away."

"And the guards?" Colonel Emilio Sangre demanded. "What happened to them?"

Sangre was a huge man, extremely tall by average Puerto Rican standards. He had a thick, broad mustache. He chewed on a fat black cigar that was grown on his own ranch in the Arecibo district and manufactured in his own factory on the outskirts of San Juan. He was sweating as he held the receiver, listening for long stretches, belching out terse questions past his fat cigar.

"We can only assume they were killed by the man you warned us about. We know that the entire villa—the laboratory, barracks, everything—was blown up within an hour after the trucks left."

"And Alto Segundo?"

"We have tripled the guard contingent. We have speeded up production as rapidly as safety factors will allow. As for the complete bomb, it is in place and already triggered for detonation at the prescribed time."

"Your safety precautions. Are they adequate?"

"More than adequate. No unauthorized personnel can so much as rattle a doorknob without the bomb being detonated. Even if there is an earthquake, the triggering device will probably—"

Colonel Sangre laughed. "Pray that there is no earthquake until we have time to make our planned visits to keep our various appointments. And no unauthorized personnel."

"Nothing can go wrong, Tranquilo. Our men have the entire building surrounded. They are stealing ideas from mainland authorities, posing as telephone repairmen, sewer workers, taxi drivers, delivery men. They have the building under constant surveillance. And they are heavily armed."

"A kind of early-warning device," the colonel said, laughing again. "And of course you are well prepared for a hasty departure in case anyone penetrates your security?"

"Oh, yes," the caller replied. "I have the helicopter you provided. It is on the roof, well concealed. And the pilot you sent with it is on call around the clock. By the time—"

"I have the picture," Colonel Sangre snapped. He took a drag on his cigar and blew the smoke at the mouthpiece. The buzzer on his desk sounded. "Excuse me," he said to his caller. He pressed a switch on the intercom. The general's secretary informed him that a man from Washington was here to see him.

The colonel grinned. He'd been expecting such a man since learning of the predawn raid on the villa laboratory. The man on the phone was only one of many to inform him of the assault.

"I have an important visitor," the colonel told his latest caller. "If you have vital news, call me. I shall do the same for you. Otherwise, the fewer calls the better."

"Sí. I understand, Tranquilo. Viva jueves."

The colonel grinned at his parting words. Viva jueves. Long live Thursday.

Thursday was two days away. The bomb was to be detonated on Thursday morning.

Unless some interference caused a premature detonation.

Or unless some very important leader had other plans in mind. Some very important leader like General Julio Pasquez. But then, the general was out of it.

"You would be better off, Menalos," Colonel Sangre said aloud to himself, "if you had hung up with the words *'Viva mañana.'* Because that is when the bomb will blow. Tomorrow. Tomorrow morning at ten o'clock. But you can't know that, can you, my friend?"

With a broad smile, the colonel spoke again to the sergeant at the other end of the intercom.

"Send in the visitor. And in five minutes, send in Colonel Balleta."

He sat back in his chair, took a deep drag on his cigar, and gazed contentedly at the ceiling.

It was going well. No matter what this pesky fly from Washington had to say, it would continue to go well.

He would see to it personally.

FOUR

Nick Carter and the attractive sergeant exchanged admiring glances. The general had good taste in women, Carter thought. Or were all the women working as secretaries at Muniz AFB beautiful? He hoped so.

"The general isn't here," she told Carter. "Colonel Emilio Sangre, the base security officer and the general's chief aide, will see you."

"Thank you." The sergeant held the general's office door open for him, and he eased through the space allowed, barely brushing her breasts. He could have avoided touching them altogether, but he could tell by the smile on her pretty face that she would have been disappointed in him. Duty compelled him, he thought wryly.

"Where's General Pasquez?" Carter asked the large man in the neat Air Force uniform once the secretary had closed the door.

"I'm Colonel Emilio Sangre. I am standing in for the general. Identification, please."

The big officer looked and acted intimidating, but Carter wasn't affected. He'd faced bigger and sterner men, but he couldn't recall just when and where. He slapped open the wallet with the special ID Hawk had arranged.

After leaving La Muda in a pickup truck driven by a

local farmer, Carter had gone directly to the apartment AXE agents had set up for him in the Old City of San Juan. If things had gone well on the mountain, the apartment would not have been necessary. But things hadn't gone well, so he now wore a natty Hupp suit and carried papers that identified him as Nicholas Carter, Federal Bureau of Investigation.

The papers, Carter mused, weren't completely phony. Hawk *had* used his real name.

Colonel Emilio Sangre seemed at first glance to be one of those unfriendly types, but Carter wouldn't act on initial impulses, on first impressions. However, he couldn't escape the unsettling feeling that something was wrong here and that someday, somewhere, he might have to tangle with this big man wearing the uniform of his country. It would not be a happy entanglement.

"Okay," Carter said, snapping the wallet shut and slipping it into the inside pocket of his well-fitting jacket. "Questions. First, where is General Pasquez? I was told to contact him on arrival."

"The general is in Washington. He is attending a conference that was scheduled months ago. I have been notified that you might arrive, and I have been instructed to provide you with assistance. That assistance is on the way."

"Assistance in what form?"

"You shall soon see. Won't you please be seated, Mr. Carter?"

They both took seats, Carter the narrow wooden chair near the window, the colonel the big, swivel, cushiony one behind the general's desk.

"What went wrong, Colonel Sangre?" Carter demanded, hard put to keep the respect due military rank in his voice. "The bomb wasn't to leave until first light."

Colonel Sangre shrugged and smiled. "Who can predict what these fools will do? Menalos is a sly dog. He may have spies in our midst. He may have had a hunch, a bad feeling. *Quien sabe?''*

"Yeah," Carter sighed. "Who knows?" He leaned forward on his hard chair. "The general's informant should know. Who is he?"

The colonel's eyes narrowed beneath bushy eyebrows. Carter tried to read the look in the man's eyes. Concern? Fear? Doubt?

"I am not privy to the general's thoughts and secrets regarding this particular matter. I know only that he has been told certain details of the theft of materials from the nuclear power plant, and of other matters. Why is it so important that you know the name of his informant?"

"Because the bastard forgot to tell the general some pretty basic facts," Carter said, his tone matching the big colonel's for pure harshness and no-nonsense pitch.

"Such as?"

"Alto Primero was one of two labs," Carter said, wondering if he should be talking with this second-string honcho at all.

"Where did you learn this?" the colonel demanded. "What do you know of a second laboratory?" The colonel seemed unable to bear the intensity of Carter's cold stare, but he maintained eye contact, obviously angered over this latest bit of news. Angered or frightened? Or both?

Carter told the colonel of the events on Alto Primero, of how the Los Bravos guard named Santiago had talked of his leaders, of the plan to detonate the bomb in downtown San Juan on Thursday morning, of the second lab in the mountains, of the limited time factor. The colonel's eyes darted around the office, from Carter to the ceiling, to the tip of his cigar, to the general's shiny desk top. The man was obviously impressed—and perhaps frightened—by Carter's intelligence and the incredible threat to the lives of everyone in the city of San Juan. But Carter was certain there was more to it. The man was nervous, like a child caught with its hand in the cookie jar.

"You cannot take this man Santiago seriously," Colonel Sangre blurted when Carter had finished with his tale of death and destruction. "All these Los Bravos maniacs are schooled in guile and treachery. This man could have told you these things to lead you away from the real issues."

"Which are?"

"It is clear to me that no Puerto Rican, not even the most fanatical follower of Los Bravos, would blow up his beloved capital city just to make the people in Washington take notice of political demands. According to the general's sources, the trucks carrying the bomb are already hiding near Caguas, fifteen miles south of San Juan. Tonight, they will continue on under cover of darkness to San Felipe on the southern coast to meet with a trawler."

"Sure," Carter said, his face bland, noncommittal. "Tell me about this trawler."

"There is little to tell," the colonel said, tapping an ash into an ashtray made from a shell casing. "Los Bravos have hired a trawler to come pick up their bomb. Why should we know much else?"

"For one thing," Carter said, "I've already checked sailing manifests. No trawler is scheduled to leave any point on the mainland or any Caribbean port in time to reach San Felipe by tomorrow morning."

The colonel grinned. "Have you checked sailing manifests for Communist vessels? Possibly those from Cuba?"

Carter returned the grin. "I see. So you think Fidel is involved. The trawler will come from Cuba, then?"

"I state it only as a possibility."

"If that's the case," Carter said, "how do your sources expect the trawler to deliver the bomb to an American port on the mainland? Trade with Cuban vessels is prohibited."

A cloud seemed to pass behind the colonel's eyes, as

though he realized that the general's "sources" hadn't been as reliable as he'd thought.

"I don't know. An exchange at sea, perhaps, to a non-Communist vessel."

"And to which port in the U.S. would this second vessel take the bomb?"

The colonel caught Carter's probing, penetrating gaze, then let his eyes glance away to the window. "We don't have that information yet. Possibly Miami. Possibly New Orleans, or one of the many ports in Mississippi or Alabama."

"Possibly," Carter said. "But your sources were wrong on the timing. They could be wrong on the destination. Santiago could have been telling the truth." Carter knew for certain that Santiago had been telling the truth. And yet. . . .

The colonel shook his head. "Intelligence in such matters can never be wholly reliable, but you can rely on one thing: that man Santiago on the mountaintop was lying, hoping to throw you off. Your next move must be to check out San Felipe and the trawler."

"Maybe," Carter said, studying the big officer with cool, unrevealing eyes. "How much do you and the general know about a man called 'Tranquilo'?"

"I cannot speak for General Pasquez," Sangre said, his eyes dropping quickly from Carter's gaze, "but I know of no such person. The word means—"

"I know what it means. I want to know the name of the man using it."

The colonel shrugged again, as though shrugging were his main conversational attribute. He seemed flustered. His big hand trembled as he reached across the desk toward a row of buttons.

"As I said, I will provide help for you, as the general ordered." He pressed the second button in the row and blurted, "Tell Colonel Balleta to come in." He turned back to Carter. "Even with the Coast Guard being ever vigilant at the U.S. ports of call, we cannot depend on them stopping that trawler. You must prevent it from ever leaving San Felipe.''

Carter was about to protest, to tell the colonel that he had no intentions of skewing off to the south coast of Puerto Rico when the real problem lay here in the city and in the second mountain laboratory called Alto Segundo, when a truly striking woman with blond hair and the uniform of a U.S. Air Force colonel entered the office. The woman had Latin features, but her eyes were a deep blue and her blond hair was swirled into an attractive chignon at the nape of her neck. She clutched her uniform cap under one arm. With barely a glance at Carter, she stopped in front of the general's desk and snapped a salute at Colonel Emilio Sangre.

The colonel smiled. ''Nicholas Carter, I want you to meet Colonel Irena Balleta, another of the general's aides. She will be your guide to San Felipe. Or, if you choose to divert your attentions elsewhere, she will do her best to provide assistance.''

Carter swallowed hard as the beautiful colonel turned to face him. She smiled and extended a small, delicate hand. He shook it, feeling something akin to an electric shock ripple up his arm.

''Call me Irena,'' she said in a husky, throaty voice that carried a kind of melody. ''And I shall call you?''

''Oh, yeah, uh, Nick,'' Carter stammered, acting as he thought he should in this situation. ''Yeah, just Nick.''

Sangre was beaming with pleasure, obviously delighted at the reaction of the FBI agent to this beautiful officer. His smile was the gratifying smile of a man who had just been proved right.

''You can trust this officer fully and implicitly,'' he told Carter. ''She knows the plans of Los Bravos. She should. Her brother is Antonio Vortez, one of the radical leaders.''

''Half brother,'' Irena corrected, still smiling up at

Carter. "My father died when I was six, and my mother married again. I detested my stepfather, Ignacio Vortez, and I hated the child he and my mother bore. I tell you this only because I don't want you to think that I have any admiration for what Antonio Vortez and his band of hoodlums are doing to our country."

There was fire in the melodic voice, fire in the deep blue eyes, fire in the small, erect, full-breasted body of Irena Balleta. Carter liked what he saw and heard. His attention was no longer on the imposing colonel, but on the incredibly beautiful and fiery woman who was one of the general's aides. Yes, the general really did have great taste in women.

Carter's shock at learning that Irena Balleta was related to the terrorist leader Antonio Vortez was short-lived. Her hatred of the man was so intense, so believable, that he accepted the fact that there was no alliance between her and Los Bravos.

And yet something was wrong in this office. Carter could sense it, feel it in the air. He'd felt this inner tingling many times in his career, and he never ignored it. He'd learned not to deny that uncanny sense of danger; it was undoubtedly why he was still alive. He'd also learned not to reveal it to others, only to sniff out the danger and eliminate it.

He released the woman's delicate but strong hand and turned to Colonel Sangre.

"You say the trawler is to pick up the bomb tomorrow morning?"

The colonel nodded. "That is my latest information."

"Then you won't mind if I use the time between now and then to do a bit of investigating. With Colonel Balleta, of course."

Sangre shrugged. Several pounds of medals clattered on his chest. "According to General Pasquez, you may do whatever you wish. Might I ask what it is you will be investigating?"

It was Carter's turn to shrug. "I'd like to look at your aerial photos of Puerto Rico's mountain terrain. And I'd like Colonel Balleta to help me look for some people."

"People?"

"Yes, people."

Carter deliberately gave no further details. It wasn't that he didn't trust Colonel Sangre. It was just that he had decided it would be better to keep as much to himself as possible. There were some things you just accepted—or rejected—on the basis of feelings.

He didn't like the feelings he had in this office.

"Keep me informed of your activities," the colonel said a bit officiously. He stood, expanded his bemedaled chest, and extended his meaty, hairy hand.

Carter shook that hand, turned, and strode from the office. Irena Balleta stood for a moment gazing at Sangre and at Nick Carter's back, then followed the spy out of the office.

"What is your problem?" she asked when they were alone in the corridor.

"No problem. Take me to the air reconnaissance office where we can look at some pictures. After that, I have some questions I'd like to ask."

"All right." She gazed for a time into the hard eyes, then turned and led him down the corridor.

Twenty minutes later, they left the headquarters building and climbed into Colonel Balleta's jeep. Carter had a folder full of photos on his lap. The lovely colonel headed the jeep toward the main gate. She drove in silence, emulating the mysterious man from Washington. Ten minutes passed. Her passenger seemed to be looking for something alongside the road. Suddenly he jerked his thumb at a side road ahead.

"Pull in there. Go a couple of hundred yards up and then stop."

Irena did as she was told, parking the jeep on an overlook with a breathtaking view of the Caribbean. Her passenger put the folder on the floor and turned to face her.

"Something's rotten," Carter said flatly. "Either Sangre is lying or the general has untrustworthy informants. Wait—don't interrupt. I know your allegiance has to be to the general, but it also has to be to Puerto Rico, to America. Am I right?"

She smiled. He got quite another feeling from looking into that lovely oval face with the deep blue eyes. He knew he would have to watch that, not let that look soften him.

"I have the feeling you're always right," she said. "Yes, my allegiance is to General Pasquez. It is also to my country. What is it you wish to tell me? What is this thing that is rotten?"

"I don't know, but I damned well intend to find out. For starters, what can you tell me about this Colonel Sangre?"

"There is nothing to tell. He is an excellent officer."

"I got the feeling that he was trying to tell me something," Carter said. "A friendly warning to me, perhaps."

The beautiful colonel laughed. "You're imagining things, Mr. Carter. Colonel Sangre is an administrative officer because, despite his powerful size, he has a terrible fear of flying, of heights. He is also the base security chief. He is a naturally suspicious man, as are you."

"Perhaps," Carter said, not satisfied with the explanation. "Look, forget Sangre. We have a lot of ground to cover and little time to do it. A lot of people are going to die if we don't get our act together. Beyond that, I can see all sorts of problems."

"Tell me about them."

"If that bomb is set off in San Juan," Carter told her, "certain people in this country—people like your half brother and that nutty physicist, Jorge Menalos—are going to try to take over. I have news for them. If that bomb goes off, the U.S. military will swarm in here so fast and so plentifully that nobody will have the upper hand. This island will be under military rule, the way it was after the Spanish-American War. I don't think you want that.''

"No.''

"All right. Work with me. Don't get bent out of shape if I say anything that might insult your general. Or your people. Will you work with me?''

"Of course. What do you want me to do?''

"We have three distinct jobs, each of them interwoven with the other. We have to find Alto Segundo, the second mountain laboratory, and halt production on any new bombs. Don't look so surprised. There *is* a second lab. The third job is to trace the pipeline of fissionable materials so that this kind of thing can never happen again. We don't necessarily have to take the jobs in that order, but we should begin by getting any information we can from anybody we can. We have about forty-eight hours before the bomb is to go off. I'll put some people on that mountain lab by sending these photos to a friend in Washington. Meanwhile, you must know some of your half brother's habits, his hangouts, his friends, his enemies. His enemies would probably help us most. I want you to give me everything you have on Antonio Vortez. He may or may not be the key, but we have to start somewhere.''

Irena pursed her lips and stared out to sea, then she turned and flashed that amazing smile again.

"I was right when I said I have the feeling you're always right. You're on the right track. Three weeks ago, two men, Diego Alvarez and Paquito Sanchez, quit Antonio's group and went into hiding. We could talk to them.''

"But you said they went into hiding.''

"I know where they are. Or at least how to get word to them that I want to talk to them.''

"Why haven't you done it before?''

"Why should I? I only learned about the bomb yesterday.''

Carter stared hard into her eyes. Was she telling the truth? He didn't know. But there was one solid, undeniable truth. This woman hated Antonio Vortez, one of the top leaders of Los Bravos. And she loved her country. He wondered, though, if she loved only Puerto Rico, or America, or both.

Carter figured he'd have to take some things on faith. For now.

"Let's go. Drive me to Isla Grande Airport so I can send these photos by private plane."

"And then?"

"And then we get you out of that uniform . . ."

He stopped, grinning at her, watching her expression run a gamut of emotions as his words were left hanging.

". . . and into civilian clothes," he finished. "Then we go after Diego Alvarez and Paquito Sanchez."

Carter said nothing more. But he caught the sigh of disappointment as Irena turned the jeep and headed back down to the main highway.

This arrangement has definite possibilities, he told himself, and he bent down to retrieve his folder so she wouldn't see his smile.

FIVE

At Isla Grande, a small airport for private planes, Carter paid well for a pilot to deliver the packet of photographs to Washington's National Airport. He wanted Colonel Irena Balleta to know that he was sending the photos, but he didn't want her to hear his conversation with Hawk.

He closed the door to the phone booth. Irena didn't seem offended, or even curious.

"What's going on?" Hawk snapped into the phone. Carter could almost see him with the cigar rolling around in his stern mouth, a look of concern on his otherwise all-business face. "We heard from General Pasquez—"

"Sir, never mind what you heard from the general," Carter said, letting his boss know right off that he didn't fully trust the general—or the general's information sources. "Here's what happened, and here's what's going to happen."

Carter told him everything that had happened and everything he had learned since leaving the *Griffith* almost twelve hours earlier. He also told Hawk about the general's faulty information.

"It may not be faulty," Hawk said. "You're pitting one dying fanatic's word against a well-organized and well-paid network of spies. We can't let that trawler business go unchecked. Or those trucks going to San Felipe.''

"We won't. What's the chopper squadron doing?''

"Do you really need the flyboys?'' Hawk asked.

Carter glanced through the glass door of the phone booth and saw Colonel Irena Balleta move around the corner of the building, heading for the airport office. Why wasn't she more curious about his phone conversation? he wondered.

"I need them,'' he said to Hawk. He told him about the photographs he was sending by private plane. "Please have them picked up at National, study them, then set up some flyover recons of the ones I've marked with red X's. After that, I want the squadron to set up aviation house-keeping on the mountain I've marked with a red circle. The commander can contact me via radio. I have mine with me.''

"Anything else?''

"Yes, sir. Put some people to watching trawler move-ments out of Cuba this afternoon and tonight. Have them check truck movements on the road from Caguas to San Felipe. And I have some names for you to run through the computer.''

He gave Hawk the name "Tranquilo,'' then added the names of Colonel Emilio Sangre, Colonel Irena Balleta, and Antonio Vortez.

"Do you want the computer info channeled through General Pasquez's office?'' Hawk asked.

"No, sir,'' Carter said. "Have it sent with the squadron commander.''

"All right. I gather you don't trust the general or anyone in his office. I won't ask why. Not now. Just keep in touch, Nick. And be careful. You could be dead wrong, you know.''

"I know. That's why I want you and the squadron to back me while I bird-dog the combat bunch. Anything else from your end?''

"No." There was a pause and a sigh. "Just take care, Nick."

Carter had learned from years of experience how to read his boss's thoughts and emotions. The old man was really worried about this one. And, Carter thought as he recalled the events of the night, he had good reason to be worried.

"I will, sir."

Carter emerged from the phone booth just as Irena was coming from the airport office. He wondered what she'd done in there, but he put the suspicion aside. He made comparisons between other women he had worked with during his long service with AXE and Colonel Irena Balleta, the career Air Force officer who looked like all the girls a guy would like to have living next door. Except for a rare few, Irena came out far ahead.

Carter had a weakness for smart, beautiful women, and they for him. But he rarely trusted them completely. And he didn't trust Irena any more than he trusted that big, mustachioed colonel who was the general's chief aide.

Yet he would be sharing the next few hectic and terrifying days with her.

"Sorry to have taken so long," he said. "Had to make certain those photos got picked up right away."

Irena said nothing until they were in the jeep, wheeling away toward the Old City.

"You arranged for an air recon from the mainland."

He glanced her way, then back to the road. "What makes you think that?"

"If I were you, I would. If I were you, I wouldn't trust Colonel Sangre or General Pasquez. I wouldn't even trust me."

"I don't."

She smiled. "It shows. But the fact is, Mr. Nicholas Carter, you have no choice."

He managed a wry grin and began to trust Irena Balleta a bit more. But not all the way. She seemed to sense this.

"What can I do to win your trust?"

"Time and performance are the best tests," he replied.
"Do you have another test in mind?"

"For one thing," she said, grinning back at him, "I
can't wait to get out of this uniform. Where do you
propose I do it?"

"The only logical place is your apartment," Carter
said, all innocence. "Unless the general's people managed to sneak some lady's civvies into the apartment
arranged for me. Last time I looked, I was fresh out of
dresses."

"But not out of electronic bugs," Irena said.

"You serious?"

"Yes. After word came that Washington had arranged
for an apartment in the Old City for a man from the
mainland, a special team went out there. That was last
night, while you were on your way up the Grande de
Loíza."

"Do you know who sent the team to the apartment?"

"Not exactly. The order had to come from the general's
office, though."

"Or from the office of base security," Carter offered.

"Yes, Colonel Sangre could have issued such an order
without the general's knowledge. I doubt that he would,
however."

"Why do you doubt it?"

"He's a climber, an ambitious leech. I don't think he'd
do anything that might backfire and put him in a bad light
with his superiors. He wants his general's star the way
some women want a tall, dark, and handsome man."

Carter grinned once more and gazed at her with a new
sparkle in his eyes. "What interesting analogies you come
up with."

"Why not? Don't tell me you're one of *those*?"

She had been striking in Air Force blue. In the nude, she
was pink and breathtaking. Carter lay on the soft bed in

her frilly bedroom and watched as she moved into the bathroom doorway. He was naked, with only a lavender sheet over his legs. She was naked, with nothing over anything. His clothing hung over a nearby chair; his small radio transceiver lay on the night table.

There had been something quaintly old-fashioned in her shyness, in her insistence that she undress in the bathroom while he got into bed alone. He liked that. What he saw in the doorway had little to do with simple likes and dislikes.

His eyes ravaged her, drank her in, digested her, savored her. His fingers could hardly wait to touch her. The rest of his body felt the same way.

When she walked, slowly, across the bedroom floor to him, he lost all feelings of guilt about taking precious time for this.

It was worth it.

And after that hellish night on Alto Primero, it was something he needed.

"Nick, you're hurt!" she exclaimed when she saw the makeshift bandage he had put on that morning. "Is it serious?"

"A mere nick," he said and smiled.

"Are you sure you should, well, exert yourself?"

He chuckled. "I have no intentions of exerting myself, woman. It is my custom to let my bedmate do all the work."

Irena giggled. "I'm the kind to fly in the face of custom, Mr. Government Agent. This is one time you work for your pleasure."

And he did. And it was good. For a time she straddled him, her full thighs gripping his lean flanks. Then, as passion rose and consumed them both, he found himself in a virtual pitched battle with eroticism. He ignored the wound on his side; the blood that oozed from the bandage and down to his groin only enhanced the feeling of pure abandonment in their lovemaking.

It ended too damned soon, in his opinion.

The feeling of urgency, of danger, returned. It always did.

He paced Irena's apartment, looking at his watch every few seconds. Time seemed to be in limbo; it seemed hours since she'd left to put the word out that she needed to talk to Diego Alvarez and Paquito Sanchez, the two men who'd defected from Los Bravos.

It had been only forty minutes.

Carter didn't like the situation. Not at all. He was accustomed to going out to dig up his own sources, make the contacts, set up the meetings. And since he didn't fully trust these military people, his dislike for the waiting was even more intense.

He felt guilty, as if he were sloughing off responsibility. He felt trapped, as though he'd allowed his dependence on others to become far too great.

But, he thought, when in Rome . . . or Puerto Rico.

She returned shortly after one o'clock, bringing food for lunch, and for thought. As they ate the food for lunch, they discussed the food for thought.

"We can't change the arrangements, Nick," she said. She'd discarded the formal "Mr. Carter." She'd begun to treat him like an old and trusted friend. And he liked it. "Both men insist they won't come here, and they won't meet at any spot they don't designate themselves."

"But you said the El Palacio restaurant was in the heart of Los Bravos territory. Why would they pick such a place?"

"Because it's the least likely place Antonio and his men would expect to find them. Diego and Paquito didn't quit Los Bravos out of fear. They quit when they learned that Antonio and the others were prepared to kill literally hundreds of thousands of people to achieve their goal."

The same reason George Pierson had protested. And it had bought George Pierson a bullet in the head.

"That brings up a question," Carter said, chewing his ham and Swiss sandwich, and washing it down with a Ricos Tres, Puerto Rico's excellent beer. "Why did Antonio and the other leaders choose such a stupid way to force Washington to act on the issue of independence? Why destroy San Juan, kill so many of their own people?"

The last person he'd questioned that way had died in his arms.

"You're forgetting something very important," Irena Balleta responded. "You have only the word of that guard at Alto Primero that San Juan is the target. The general insists—"

"I know what he insists. Let's assume that I'm right. If the target *is* San Juan, Los Bravos would be killing their own people. How would that carry a message to the American government in Washington?"

Irena nodded. "You know, you may be right. Setting off the bomb in San Juan would provide a strong message. They'd be saying to the American government, 'Look at how willing our people are to die to gain independence. They are willing to die to the last man, woman, and child to break the slave ties with the United States.' That would be their message—that would be why they might set off the bomb in San Juan."

"And what is your opinion?"

Her pretty face flushed with deep feeling. "I think they are all a bunch of stupid fools."

"Where would you set off the bomb?"

She threw him a sharp look, as though he'd said something sacrilegious.

"I would not set it off at all. There are other ways."

"Political ways?"

"Yes, and others. There could be statehood."

He looked into those deep blues. Yes, she seemed to be

telling the truth. She favored statehood, which was, indeed, what most of Puerto Rico seemed to favor.

"It's time," Carter said, finishing his beer and rising from the table. "Let's go and meet your friends and see what they have to say."

"You have weapons? Just in case?"

Carter thought of Wilhelmina in his left armpit, of Hugo strapped to his arm, of Pierre high on his inner thigh.

"I have weapons," he said. "All I need."

Wilhelmina was a part of his hand when he had to use it. And he had the distinct feeling, as they left Irena's apartment and drove off in the jeep, that he would definitely have to use it that afternoon.

But not, he hoped, before he had what he needed from Diego Alvarez and Paquito Sanchez.

SIX

The feeling that he was being led into a trap stayed with Nick Carter as Irena circled the block after passing the El Palacio restaurant in Plaza de Colombo.

The bevy of thugs sitting at the sidewalk tables didn't lessen the feeling.

Irena parked the jeep two blocks away, and they walked back to the restaurant, entering through the rear. Two men sat at a table in a far corner where there was little light.

Carter, who had changed into a sporty, "touristy" outfit, gave then a quick glance. He saw a great deal in that glance. The man on the right was nervously lighting a cigarette. The man on the left chewed on an unlit cigar, reminding Carter of a dark and diminutive David Hawk. Both men were small and brown, with dark hair and in need of shaves. They wore blue jeans, tattered, gaily colored shirts, and sloppy tennis shoes.

Irena strode right to the table. Both men jumped as though they'd been shot.

The colonel was even more striking in her civilian clothes; the full white blouse and flaring navy skirt did marvelous things for her figure. Her hair had been combed out, and it hung in generous waves almost to her waist. She'd put an orchid above her left ear.

As delicious and as inviting as she looked, she still scared the hell out of the two men when she breezed up to their table.

Carter followed quickly, not giving the men a chance to bolt. He sat beside the man on the left, the one with the rolling, twitching, unlit cigar. It was Diego Alvarez. Across from him, Paquito Sanchez eyed Carter suspiciously and lit another cigarette to go with the one already glowing in an ashtray.

Carter began firing questions, but Diego Alvarez held up a bony hand.

"*Por favor, señor*. First, a bottle of wine."

"I thought you were in a hurry."

"We are." The man grinned. "But there is always time for wine, no?"

"*Sí.*" Carter ordered wine, bided time while the waiter filled four glasses, then repeated his barrage of questions: "Where is the downtown building where the bomb has been taken? Is there any truth to the report that the bomb is to be taken to San Felipe to be put aboard a trawler? Where is the second mountaintop laboratory, Alto Segundo? Is it true that the bomb will be set off at eleven A.M. Thursday? Is it true that the triggering device is set up to detonate at the slightest interference? Who is the main contact for fissionable materials and how do Los Bravos get them?"

Diego Alvarez again held up his hand.

"*Por favor, señor*. In good time. First we savor the wine."

They savored a lot of wine. Two bottles later, when Carter was at the end of his patience and ready to kill the dark little men, Diego Alvarez suddenly began to talk.

"We begin at the beginning," he said, speaking slowly and deliberately. "Eight months ago, a wealthy man by the name of Jesus Damorcito came to see Antonio Vortez in our headquarters, not far from here. You know this Jesus Damorcito?"

Carter shook his head; he'd never heard the name.

"You should know this man, *señor*. He is very wealthy. He has many friends in high places. He can get you anything you want. He has a villa near Trujillo Alto. A very splendid place. A fortress, in fact."

"Is it the second laboratory?"

Both men laughed. Nervous laughs. They looked around the restaurant, toward the bright open entrance, through the unsavory-looking men sitting at the sidewalk tables.

"Jesus Damorcito is too intelligent for such direct involvement. His reason for visiting Antonio Vortez was to tell him that he could arrange, for a price, to provide fiss—fish—"

"Fissionable?"

"*Sí*. Those kind of materials. With them and a couple of scientists who know the workings of atomic bombs, Antonio Vortez could have such powerful weapons. *Dios, amigo!* The wine is all gone. My voice dries up and cracks. I can speak no more."

Carter ordered two more bottles. He even pushed his filled but untouched glass under Diego Alvarez's nose. Both men drank, sighed, belched. Alvarez continued.

"Well, *señor*, we began a series of bank robberies to obtain the great amount of money this Jesus Damorcito demanded for his atomic material—whatever it is you call it . . ."

"Plutonium," Carter supplied. "Where and how was Jesus Damorcito to obtain this material?"

"The nuclear plant at Punta Jiguero, of course," Alvarez said. "He has spies inside the plant. They told him that the plutonium produced by the reactor fuel was sometimes taken out on trucks carrying waste materials. Damorcito's spies would tell him when the plutonium was on the trucks, then he would arrange hijacking.

"And then . . . ah, what did we do then? Ah, yes, we got the money and paid this Damorcito. Then we recruited the two men, George Pierson and Jorge Menalos. Do you know that Jorge in Spanish is George in English? We recruited two Georges.''

Paquito Sanchez began to laugh at the hilarious fact that two Georges had been recruited. His laughter was infectious, but only to his dark little friend. Both men began a drunken laughter that had others in the restaurant looking their way.

Carter was the nervous one now. Wine had eradicated fear and nervousness in the two defectors. Alvarez had become drunkenly garrulous. It might take hours to get anything of real value from these wine-loving ex-Bravos.

But the laughter stopped as suddenly as it had begun. Diego Alvarez took a deep drink of wine, wiped the stubble around his mouth, and began to speak again.

''The first laboratory, on Alto Primero, soon proved inadequate for all the work that needed to be done. A second one was set up at an old building on top of—''

The street outside exploded in a squeal of tires from several heavy vehicles. Firing from automatic weapons boomed across Plaza de Colombo.

Carter, his hand already on the butt of the Luger, snapped his head around to look through the bright entrance. The thugs at the sidewalk tables began to scatter. Two of them fell, blood gushing from their mouths and chests.

Irena jumped to her feet, her eyes also glued to the entrance. Carter followed her gaze and saw several men in paramilitary garb sweep in an arc around the restaurant front. They were firing point-blank into the sidewalk tables.

''My God, it's Antonio!'' Irena shouted. ''Come! Out the back way!''

Carter followed her frantic gaze and saw a tall, skinny man with a .45 in his hand. He was directing the rifle-carrying men into position. Antonio Vortez was a dark man with a full beard and penetrating eyes. He reminded Carter of a young Fidel Castro. Castro at his angriest.

Carter looked back at the two defectors, knowing he

needed them. He tried to yank Diego Alvarez to his feet, but the man was so drunk he wasn't even aware that he was in danger. Across from him, Paquito Sanchez seemed to have gone into a stupor.

"Antonio has seen us, Nick!" Irena shouted. "There's no time to take Diego with us! Come! We can still get out the back way!"

But Carter was determined. He jerked Wilhelmina from her holster and took dead aim on a Los Bravos soldier who was now wading through dead bodies and fleeing patrons, entering the restaurant.

The Killmaster fired. The fierce, hurtling 9mm parabellum slug quickly closed the distance between gun and man, and entered the man's head. Carter saw a shower of blood, brains, bone, and hair fly away from that onrushing skull. The Luger's explosion hung in the air.

Carter was aiming at another man when an automatic weapon let go with an ear-shattering roar inside the restaurant proper. One of Vortez's men had made it inside. He was behind an overturned table, and he was looking directly at Carter and Irena.

"Come on, Nick!" Irena shouted. "You can't fight them all!"

The man with the automatic rifle proved her point when he swept the dark corner with a vicious blast of crashing steel.

Diego Alvarez was literally jerked from Carter's grip. His body, riddled with bullets, tumbled over the table and slammed against the wall.

Carter fired twice in the direction of the gunman, then turned to run after Irena and found himself tangled in the bloody body of Paquito Sanchez. The quiet little man was still taking slugs as Carter stepped over him and fled down the dark hallway to the rear door.

He hated to run, hated to give up the battle. But the weaponry and manpower were too much for a solitary Luger.

Fueling Carter's anger was the growing suspicion that

Irena had set up this trap. But had it been a trap for him or for the two defectors?

He put all such thoughts aside and bolted through the rear door after Irena. He expected to see her running hard down the alley.

She wasn't running.

She was sprawled on the cobblestones, blood making an ugly mess of her white blouse. The orchid she'd worn over her ear was lying beside her. Her long blond hair was matted with blood.

He heard footsteps from behind. Los Bravos men were coming down the hallway toward the rear door.

Carter scooped up the wounded woman and started off down the alley. He wondered if he were making a mistake here. Carrying her—even though she wasn't very heavy—slowed him dangerously. His own wound complained bitterly. But he couldn't leave her.

He put on a burst of speed and ducked around the corner at the end of the alley. As he ran toward where Irena had parked the jeep, he heard sirens, more gunshots, then heard an explosion that was unmistakably a grenade.

Los Bravos were putting on quite a show.

A block from the jeep, he stopped. The jeep was ablaze, parts of it strewn all over the street.

Escape was impossible now.

And Irena was bleeding profusely. Some of it, he suspected, was his own blood.

Carter cut down another alley off the plaza and eased into a doorway. He gripped Irena's unconscious body, his Luger at the ready.

He had enough slugs left to blow away the first few terrorists. He waited, wondering how many would come.

The sirens screamed louder. Tires squealed in the streets around the plaza. Carter watched from his narrow vantage point and waited for Los Bravos.

A jeep rumbled past the alley entrance and made a sudden stop. Carter had caught the lettering on the side:

U.S. Navy. He'd seen the four big shore patrol officers in the jeep.

They were between him and Vortez's men. He heard the distinctive fire of .45 automatics and knew that the SPs were driving back "the ferocious ones."

Now was his chance.

He carried Irena to the end of the alley, gauged the distance to the Navy jeep, and ran like hell.

The key was in the ignition. He placed Irena in the passenger seat, looped the seat belt around her, and hopped in. The bleeding seemed to have stopped. He started the jeep's engine and made a U-turn. As he streaked past Irena's burning jeep, he heard the whine of bullets above his head.

He jammed the accelerator to the floor.

Twenty minutes later, he was through the barrio of Pueblo and was heading for the narrow strip of highway that would take them to Trujillo Alto.

But first, he knew he had to find a doctor for Irena. He'd made a quick inspection of her wound. A bullet had caught her in the side, near her left breast. Thankfully, there were no other wounds.

Irena needed a doctor, but not here, not in San Juan. Los Bravos and the authorities alike would be after him now. Carter recalled his previous trips to Puerto Rico and knew that there were villages in the mountains. He'd find a doctor there.

The jeep began to climb. Dark, purplish mountains loomed ahead. Irena began to stir.

"Where are we going?" she asked, her voice faint.

He glanced over at her. She was upright in the seat, no longer straining against the belt. Blood again oozed from her wound, and he gave her his handkerchief.

"Here, press this to your side. I don't think the bullet is in there. You have a flesh wound. You must have fainted."

"I did," she admitted. "I felt something sting me as we

were running down that hallway. I saw the blood when I got to the alley. The sight of it made me pass out.''

He grinned. ''You don't happen to know of any doctors up this way, do you?''

She had already glanced around and found the answer to her own question. They were high above the city now, heading toward Trujillo Alto, toward the villa of the wealthy man named Jesus Damorcito, the contact for fissionable materials.

Perhaps he was the key to opening this Pandora's box of terror.

Terror, it seemed, had replaced gold—and even time—as the rich port's most precious commodity.

''I have a friend,'' Irena said, slipping the handkerchief under her blouse and pressing it against the wound. ''Just before we get to Trujillo Alto, take a road to the left, toward Carolina. My friend isn't a doctor, but she has medical supplies. Her name is Maria Escobar.''

Carter speeded up.

The road was becoming increasingly steep, increasingly tortuous.

But he knew where he had to go now.

He'd never been to Trujillo Alto, but he'd studied maps of the entire island since his briefing by Hawk.

He'd get Irena's wound patched up.

And then he'd get down to some really serious business.

''Better speed up if you can,'' Irena said, turning in the seat to watch the winding road behind. ''They've caught up with us. That's Antonio's car.''

Carter had been checking the rearview mirror but had seen nothing. He checked it now. Sure enough, someone was following in a huge limousine. Carter would have bet his life that the limousine contained Los Bravos men. And that it was bulletproof.

He wouldn't have lost the bet. As for his life, that was another thing.

The limousine was closing fast.

SEVEN

Nick Carter hated car chases. Whether he was the pursuer or the pursued, he'd just as soon not be involved in such fruitless, frustrating races.

And it was hardly a race this time. The limo was considerably faster than the jeep, even on the twisting, turning, narrow road up the mounain.

To make matters worse, Irena had fainted again. Her unconscious body strained against the seat belt. A violent turn could send her jetting out into space.

To certain death.

Maybe certain death waited for both of them, Carter thought.

His most effective weapon right now had to be his wits. The Luger would be a peashooter against that armored limo, and Pierre's gas would dissipate on the brisk mountain wind. Even if he tried to ram the limo off a cliff, the powerful motor under that long hood was more than a match for the jeep.

The enemy had the power, the speed, the armor, the weaponry. And they were, figuratively, in the catbird seat as the pursuers.

Carter had to turn all that around.

He had to place himself—and Irena—in even greater jeopardy if he were to gain the upper hand. There was

57

danger enough on the steep, twisting road. High cliffs were at each violent turn.

But the greater jeopardy—the greater danger—was in speeding *down* the mountain, not up.

Carter picked a spot far ahead, where the road widened to an overlook on the left. Alongside the black macadam was a light patch of sandy soil where cars had parked, where people had looked out over the hills and the city to the distant ocean.

The spot wasn't large enough to make a U-turn. Not by normal U-turn standards.

By Nick Carter's standards, learned from having driven racing cars with the pros, it was wide enough. Just.

Or so he hoped.

He glanced at the rearview mirror and saw that the limo was a half mile back. He keyed on the wide spot ahead and gauged his speed. He'd have to make the turn to his left.

It was dangerous that way. But any other way was certain failure.

He'd have to hug the wall of the mountain on his right and, at the proper time, spin the wheel all the way to his left and hit the brakes and accelerator pedal at all the right times.

Centrifugal motion would fling Irena toward the right, toward open space beyond the cliff. If that seat belt broke. . . .

Carter had no time to dwell on that. He was at the point of no return. He eased to the right and heard the screech of metal as the jeep scraped the wall. He was using every inch of available space.

Now.

He spun the wheel to the left. The big tires groaned and complained, cut into gravel, dug into sand, hit the hot asphalt again.

Brake. Accelerate. Turn. Brake. Accelerate.

Carter felt the G-forces working on his own body. The jeep was spinning wildly around in what race drivers called the "moonshiners' turn."

The rear wheels spun across the macadam and spat up dirt in the parking area. Rocks and sand flew over the cliff's edge.

The forces grew more violent, more insistent. Carter felt his hands being torn from the wheel. Felt his buttocks being flung from the seat.

Brake. Accelerate. Brake. Accelerate.

The jeep came to within inches of the cliff's edge. The tires bucked and spat. The engine labored and roared.

Carter was facing the limo now and saw it slowing down. He even saw a puzzled look on the face of the driver.

A window went down. An automatic rifle snapped into view.

Accelerate.

With a grinding of gears and a spitting of dirt, the jeep lurched out of the parking area, heading downhill. Zipping past the limo, Carter saw tongues of flame and heard the cracking rifle, then saw angry faces.

One of those faces was the bearded, angry countenance of Antonio Vortez.

Through the rearview mirror, Carter saw the limo come to a screeching halt and begin to seesaw back and forth in the road to make its own turn. The jeep zipped around a hairpin turn, and Carter lost sight of the limo.

Okay, he thought. *Step one completed. Irena's still with me, none the worse for wear.*

He was now ready for his next move.

Carter hadn't been idle on the way up the mountain. He'd seen numerous places where an ambush could be laid, given the time and opportunity.

He'd made the opportunity. Now all he needed was the time.

Carter speeded up, racing dangerously down the twisting road and listening to the complaints of the tires on the tight turns. Dirt and rocks were flung into the air as the jeep went perilously close to the cliff's edge on its breakneck plunge down the mountain.

"My God, what are you doing?"

It was Irena. Her voice, still faint, was high with fear. She was conscious again, gripping the door and staring at the onrushing road ahead.

"Buying time."

"But we were going *up* the mountain. How did you shake them?"

Carter grinned. "I'll tell you all about it sometime. Right now, I've got a plan."

He stormed the jeep into a shallow dip in the road. Ahead, he remembered the road topped a rise and made a sharp turn to the right, at the edge of an exceptionally high cliff. Carter stopped in the dip, slammed the gear in reverse, and backed the jeep off the road and into a small hollow. Irena ducked as the limbs of pine and palm trees scraped across the top of the jeep.

"Stay here, out of sight," he commanded.

He leaped from the jeep and ran up the shallow incline to where the road made its turn. He literally yanked bushes up by the roots and piled them in the road at the turn. From down the hill, it looked as though the road did not turn, but merely went over a rise and continued straight.

Nick Carter kept ripping and tearing at bushes, even hauling down a great limb to pile it on the road.

He was about to run back to the jeep, to hide with Irena, when he heard the limo's racing engine from above. Antonio Vortez was indeed angry. He was plunging recklessly down the mountain road, eager to catch the jeep that had eluded him.

Carter calmly stepped into the bushy wall he'd created and stood there watching.

The limousine raced down the steep incline, then dipped and swayed when it reached the shallow spot in the road. The big car seemed to hover for a moment as the driver sensed uncertain conditions ahead.

Then it roared up the incline, flashed past Carter, and took to the air.

Carter stepped from the bushes and watched it go.

The limo actually flew for several hundred feet straight out into the air. Then it nosed over and began hurtling end over end toward the valley floor far below.

Carter lit a cigarette, watching and waiting.

He didn't see the impact. He heard a soft *whomp* echo up through the valley, then saw the enormous fireball as the gas tank exploded.

The following concussive boom literally shook the leaves on the trees and bushes around him.

Four more down. Many, many more to go. Either that, or thousands would be incinerated in a fiery blast that not even the gods desired to contemplate. Not even the god of war.

This wasn't a war on the part of Los Bravos. It was mass murder. It was criminal.

Nick Carter had to stop them and their hideous plan. Any way he could.

EIGHT

In the Amalgamated Press and Wire Services Building on Dupont Circle in the heart of Washington, D.C., the short, white-haired man paced nervously back and forth in his office. A glowing black stub, the remnant of a cigar that had been fired up only minutes before, chugged out thick smoke—like a steam locomotive climbing a particularly steep hill.

The man was David Hawk, the brilliant mind behind AXE. His thick, sturdy, fireplug-shaped torso and his boundless energy belied his age. Hawk was past sixty, but he had the vitality and drive of a man more than a decade younger. On this particular afternoon, he was brimming with nervous energy, anger, and—yes—fear.

Intelligence reports had been filtering in through Amalgamated, the cover organization for AXE, by the minute. Hawk didn't care for any of the reports or what they portended. His premier Killmaster had been in difficulties before, many times, but Hawk couldn't recall when they had been stacked so decidedly against success.

Not only had the special squadron failed to scramble as ordered—because the President was attending some luncheon in his honor and wasn't available to countersign the order—but Carter had virtually disappeared from the scene in Puerto Rico.

There had been a shootout in a sidewalk café in the heart of the Old City, and Carter had been seen fleeing the site with a wounded woman, a group of Los Bravos in hot pursuit. There had been a report of a vehicle mishap in the mountains—a car or jeep plunging over a steep precipice and an explosion of that car or jeep—but there were no reports yet as to whether Carter and the mysterious woman were victims of that accident.

Even if Carter survived, which Hawk had seriously begun to doubt, he was on the wrong track. Hawk had spoken to General Julio Pasquez in person, dragging him from his conference at the Pentagon for that purpose.

"There is no denying my sources," the general had said. "Your man is—how do you say it?—barking up the wrong tree. The bomb is to be picked up by trawler at dawn tomorrow and taken to a city in the United States. This business about San Juan is a ploy, a diversion."

The general's information jibed with what Hawk had learned from the ComSat people. A Russian trawler had left Tierra del Fuego, Cuba, two days before and was now on a heading for San Felipe, Puerto Rico, making eight knots. It would reach San Felipe well before dawn tomorrow.

What's more, the trawler had special passengers. Twenty top Communist leaders from Russia and Cuba had gone aboard hours before the trawler had sailed. Although there was no hard data that Los Bravos were backed by the Communists, this new development boded no good. In the aftermath of an atomic blast—either in the States or San Juan—the Communists could contribute hugely to further confusion to make the takeover of Puerto Rico by unfriendly forces virtually a piece of cake.

Things were becoming, to say the least, a mess.

Nick Carter needed to know what Hawk now knew. The only way to get the information to him was first to find out where he was and then to get the squadron released to reach him via radio—or to arrange a meet on a remote mountaintop.

But there were big holes in the plan.

Carter might be dead. Even if he were alive, there was an outside chance that the squadron commander wouldn't be able to raise him on the special radio, either to impart information or to arrange a meet. And, of course, the President was still out of reach. The squadron wouldn't even leave its billet at Miami International Airport without the President's okay.

Hawk snatched up the telephone again. His secretary, Ginger Bateman, responded.

"Call the Avalon Room at the Biltmore again. Ask for the President's press secretary."

"Shall I tell him Amalgamated Press and Wire Services are calling?"

"No. Tell him someone is calling about a bomb threat. That should get us some action!"

Technically, Hawk wasn't lying. He was just shading the angle a bit. He had to get the President on the line, had to get that squadron moving. Otherwise, N3 was a dead duck.

If he wasn't already.

The buzzer sounded in the office of General Julio Pasquez. Colonel Sangre pressed the intercom button. The voice of the pretty sergeant blared in the room.

"Señor Menalos is on the line, Colonel. Shall I tell him you're—"

"Tell him nothing," the colonel cut in, touching a match to a sleek Cuban cigar. "I'll take the call."

Menalos came on the line. His voice sounded shaky, frightened.

"He's getting close," he said. "Vortez failed at El Palacio."

"I see. Give me details."

Menalos described the fiasco at El Palacio, telling how
Antonio Vortez, acting on an anonymous tip, had raided
the restaurant with a squad of Los Bravos men with orders
to kill the American agent and the defectors. How the
main target got away, how the defectors were killed, how
Vortez was certain that one of his men wounded Irena
Balleta. How Carter had carried her to safety. How the
appearance of Navy SPs foiled attempts to finish Carter
off.

"But didn't Vortez set up a pursuit?" the colonel demanded.

"That's where the real trouble starts," Menalos said.
"He and three men went after the Navy jeep the FBI man
had commandeered. We haven't heard from them since.
We have reports, however, of a terrific explosion in a
valley off the road to Trujillo Alto. We can only fear the
worst. This Carter is a sly person. We have underesti-
mated him."

The colonel puffed and thought. "Let us assume that he
and Irena got away. Let us assume that Irena was
wounded. Where would they go? And why were they
heading for Trujillo Alto in the first place?"

"I think the defectors must have told them about
Damorcito, and they were heading for his place. That's
what I think."

"All right. Keep calm and guard the bomb. I will
handle matters from this end. Is your rooftop helicopter
still waiting to take you away before eleven on Thursday?"

"Of course. Don't you have one waiting for you?"

The colonel coughed and tapped a long ash into his
ashtray. "Of course. Just do your part. I will do mine."

"One thing, Tranquilo," the Los Bravos leader said.
"I don't want Irena hurt. It wasn't meant that she be shot
in that raid at El Palacio. Someone got reckless."

"And what is your interest in Colonel Irena Balleta?
You hardly know her. You have seen her only a few times,

when I've had her deliver certain papers to you at your headquarters and at the laboratories. Even then, she didn't know who you really were, or what was going on at the places where she was making the deliveries.''

Menalos laughed. ''I don't like to see great beauty destroyed.''

And yet, the colonel thought, *we are going to destroy much of the great beauty of San Juan. And many beautiful people who live there.* But he said:

''She will not be hurt.''

He knew he was lying. It was a painful lie. When Sangre hung up, he lifted the receiver again and dialed a number. He called on his own, without going through the secretary. There was almost a choke in his voice as he gave the kill order on Nick Carter and Irena Balleta. He admired the woman, but there was no other way. She had to die with the troublesome man from Washington. He knew where Irena would direct Carter, now that she was wounded. He knew of Irena's friend near Carolina.

''Target is the Escobar farm, three miles west of Carolina,'' he said when he had his contact on the line. ''There is a white farmhouse with a red barn nearby. The house and barn are located at the base of a high butte on the north. Send out a mortar team and destroy the place and everyone in it.''

The colonel made a second call.

''It is time for Jesus Damorcito to go,'' he said to the listener. ''His cover might have been blown by the two defectors. Make the necessary preparations. I want no witnesses to survive, no reports that the aircraft used on his villa might be military.''

Colonel Sangre made a third call.

''Contact the captain of the trawler,'' he belched into the receiver. ''Tell him to increase speed. He must be at San Felipe well before dawn. The special passengers must—repeat, *must*—be at San Juan Exports in the city before ten A.M. tomorrow.''

He hung up, leaned back in his chair, and blew a great
arrow of cigar smoke at the ceiling.

"You are clever, Nick Carter," he said aloud. "Very
clever. But you won't survive the attack on the farmhouse
near Carolina. You shouldn't have survived the attack at
El Palacio. Damn you for that. You have put Irena in great
jeopardy. She also cannot survive the attack on the farmhouse, and that is a pity, a waste."

As certain as he was that Carter and Irena would die in
that attack, the colonel began to have doubts. Carter was
lucky. And resourceful. He might survive. If he
did. . . .

The colonel made one more call. More than a thousand
miles away, a feminine hand picked up a receiver.

"Federal Bureau of Investigation," its owner said po-
litely.

"I am calling for General Julio Pasquez, Muniz Air
Force Base, Puerto Rico," the colonel said just as po-
litely. "I have a message for an agent by the name of
Nicholas Carter. Tell him to report to the general immediately at Muniz. I repeat, it is urgent and imperative
that the general meet with him personally."

"I'm sorry, sir," the woman said after checking a
roster of FBI operatives. "We have no agent by that
name."

"Conduct a search," the colonel said. "I'm certain you
will find him."

The colonel hung up, knowing that wheels would turn
rapidly now. He smoked furiously on his cigar.

"Yes, Señor Carter, you are clever," he said, "but you
are not invincible. You have crossed paths with Tranquilo, who is far more clever. And Tranquilo *is* invincible."

Smiling, the colonel looked at his watch. It was six
o'clock.

"In just sixteen hours," he said, addressing an imagi-
nary Nick Carter, "the bomb will destroy most of this
beautiful city. The explosion will not only set the timer for

my plan to take over Puerto Rico, it will eliminate my
debts to the lousy Communists who think of me as their
next puppet. All those with whom I've had dealings will
be in the city then, at San Juan Exports. I will be
elsewhere.

"If you survive all else that I have in mind for you, Nick
Carter, I hope you too will be in the city at 10 A.M.
tomorrow.

"To share the same fate as Jorge Menalos and those
stupid Communists."

NINE

It was seven o'clock when Carter pulled the jeep into the barnyard of a white farmhouse near Carolina. He surveyed the area. Beyond a red barn was a high butte. Cold eyes studied that butte.

Irena stirred beside him. He was about to pick her up when he saw the woman on the porch. She held an enormous double-barreled shotgun.

"Who are you?" the woman demanded in a voice that could have come from a crow. She wore a flowered housedress, worn and patched from use and age.

"A friend," he called out. "This is Irena Balleta. She's been wounded."

"Irena!" the woman cried. She dropped the gun on the porch and ran down the steps.

Carter saw the look of utter concern on the woman's face. She was middle-aged, but sun and wind had left deep wrinkles on her brown face. Her work-worn hands touched Irena and pushed back a lock of hair. She let out a stream of curses and carried Irena into the house.

The woman lay Irena on a bed and bustled past Carter to the kitchen. She returned with a basin of hot water, a first aid kit, and a pair of scissors.

"Wait in the front room," she commanded. "This is women's work."

Carter was ready to oblige. He didn't mind the idea of sitting quietly by himself for a while. But it apparently wasn't women's work. He'd no sooner reached the front room when he heard a thump in the bedroom. He hurried back to the bedroom and imagined what had happened. The woman had cut away Irena's bloody blouse and brassiere, had seen the gaping gash just below her left breast, and had fainted.

Carter lugged Maria Escobar to the front room couch, then went back to tend to Irena. The wound wasn't as bad as it looked. He cleaned away the dried blood and applied hydrogen peroxide against infection.

The lovely colonel was bare from the waist up, and Carter did his best to keep his eyes on the wound as he applied mercurochrome and began to tape on a bandage. Irena was spectacularly beautiful.

She was awake now. Her deep blue eyes studied his. He leaned down and gently kissed her, then pulled away.

"Is it bad?" she asked. "The wound?"

"No. Superficial. But you lost a lot of blood. I'm going to leave you with your friend while I—"

"No," she blurted. She tried to sit up but fell back. "Wait. Wait a few minutes for me to gather strength. Maria can give us some food, and then I'll be strong enough to go with you. I must . . ."

Carter hesitated. He didn't want to wait. There was no time. His sense of danger was vibrating.

Twice he'd been fingered for death, twice betrayed.

Los Bravos were in a hurry to eliminate the one man who was investigating this bomb business, perhaps because time was of the essence. Perhaps the bomb wasn't to be detonated on Thursday.

Perhaps they were to move sooner. Perhaps Carter was getting too close, threatening an already tight timetable.

Irena could be of help. She certainly had guts, this one.

He admired her even though he didn't trust—he cut off such thoughts.

Admiration was one thing. Trust was another.

"I will heat up some soup," Maria Escobar said softly from the doorway.

They ate in the kitchen. Irena wore a worn but clean blouse of Maria's. Her bra had been destroyed by the scissors. Her ample breasts filled the flower-printed blouse; her nipples, high and erect, showed through the material. Carter found it difficult to concentrate on his food.

He was eager to leave, impatient to get to the villa of Jesus Damorcito before dark. Time could be running out. If he could force Damorcito to talk, he would be able to gain some time.

That infallible sixth sense warned him that staying here much longer was dangerous. He felt that something was happening outside.

He stood up. "I'm going, Irena. Alone."

"No!" She was on her feet, wavering unsteadily. She forced herself to stop swaying. "I'm fine now. I will go with you."

"Please, child," her friend said, her crow's voice soft and soothing now. "This is a wise and brave man. Listen to him."

"I must go," Irena protested. She walked to the doorway leading to the front room. "See, I'm fine. I can walk. The weakness is gone."

Carter puzzled over her vehemence. Why was it so important that she go along? She'd done her military duty, worked hard as his guide and aide, and had taken a painful bullet in her side. Why did she want to go above and beyond the call of duty?

He'd never find out if he left her here.

"All right," he said. Ostensibly, there wouldn't be any real trouble at Damorcito's villa. Just a small conference with the man who sold the fissionable materials to Los

Bravos. "But you have to walk to the jeep on your own."

She did. A bit wobbly, but without help. Carter strapped her into her seat. They waved to Maria, who stood on the porch shaking her head and affectionately cackling her objections in that crow's voice.

"She's a good friend to have," Carter said as he headed the jeep out of the barnyard toward the road to Trujillo Alto.

"She is more than a friend. My parents died when I was quite young. Maria Escobar raised me. I owe her everything."

Carter headed out, driving down the long lane past the barn. He checked Wilhelmina, still leathered in the holster under his arm. He patted his jacket pocket for the transceiver Hawk had provided.

It was gone!

He started to ask Irena if she had seen it, but he knew it was hopeless. It must have flown from his pocket back when he'd made that "moonshiners' turn" on the mountain road south of San Juan.

"Dammit," he cursed under his breath. They had reached the end of Maria Escobar's lane when the first explosion came. Carter guessed mortar. A column of smoke and flame belched from the white farmhouse.

The woman was no longer on the porch.

A second explosion came. The barn went up in flames. Irena screamed.

Carter's eyes, full of anger and pain, scanned the butte while Irena continued to scream and stare at the smoke and flames.

He saw them—two dark shadows—moving the mortar to another spot to send more rounds into the burning ranch.

"Stay here!" he shouted as he jumped from the jeep and jammed a new clip into his Luger.

"I must go to her—to Maria!" Irena cried.

"It's too late! She's dead!"

Carter took the ignition keys to make certain Irena didn't drive the jeep into that inferno. He took off at a dead run, up the side of the butte.

Halfway up, there was no running to be done. It was all climbing. Maybe the men had already fled, maybe not. As he neared the top, another explosion from the vicinity of the ranch confirmed their presence.

Carter pulled himself onto a wide ledge as a double explosion shook the ground beneath his feet. He saw the mortar team dead ahead, moving to still another position. A tall man and a short man.

Wilhelmina spoke.

In rapid fire, two 9mm parabellum hunks of lead crashed from the barrel of the Luger. Their courses had already been ordained by the deadly aim of the man who had dispatched them.

The first slug caught the tall man in the left eye. His arms flew upward. The mortar crashed to the ground. The short man was turning as his death approached. It caught him just below the left ear. His head snapped back. The metal case of shells he'd been carrying dropped with a crunch.

Both were dead, a result of Nick Carter's anger. Carter wished that he'd merely wounded them, at least one of them. These Los Bravos killers could be made to talk.

But anger had made him deadly. He could still see that kind woman standing on the porch in the dusk, affectionately admonishing them.

Each of the two men had machetes. They no doubt planned to leave one to show that they'd committed the daring act of blowing a wonderful woman to bits.

No. They really hadn't been after the woman, after Maria Escobar. They'd been after him, Nick Carter. And Irena Balleta. But the results were the same. They'd killed a woman who'd worked her fingers to the bone eking out an existence in this mountain terrain, rearing a fine young woman who had become an Air Force colonel.

Another innocent dead. One of thousands yet to die.

"Two can play the token game," he said to the sprawled corpses.

He broke the shiny machete blades over a rock, then jammed a 9mm cartridge between the dead lips of each of the hit men.

When he returned to the jeep, Irena was crying softly into her hands. Carter comforted her, convincing her that it would be self-torture to return to the ranch. He headed the jeep out again, heading for Trujillo Alto.

For the man named Jesus Damorcito.

His anger grew with each turn of the big whining tires.

Jesus Damorcito, a rotund little man with the pink, pretty face of an infant, stood at the window of his study and watched evening come to the mountain. When the sunset had dwindled to pale, drab colors, he turned and strode on short, pink legs to his enormous mahogany desk.

The study, on the third floor of the sprawling villa that had once been occupied by a Spanish prince, was huge and sumptuous. Its walls were paneled in African ebony, much of it covered by silk tapestries Damorcito had bought from China, back in the years when trade with China was forbidden. Stolen Picassos and other treasures hung against the ebony, between the tapestries. A carpet of ermine and mink covered the floor. Four crystal chandeliers illuminated all that richness.

Damorcito himself was a continuation of the decor. His short, pudgy frame was decked out in Pierre Cardin slacks and jacket, a Halston silk blouse with dainty ruffles at neck and wrists, and a pair of white lambskin Gucci loafers. Even his forest green socks carried the name of a fashion expert, but Damorcito had forgotten who.

As he leaned over his desk to study the contents of a huge metal strongbox, the diamond stickpin in his designer scarf caught the light of the chandeliers and sent it spiriting to all points of the room. Well-manicured fingers, heavy with diamond and emerald rings, lifted a fancy ledger from the strongbox and spread it on the desk. The fingers rifled through pages of neat penmanship until they came to a blank. Damorcito dipped a quill into a gold inkwell and began to write:

> *One more competitor is gone. Antonio Vortez. Only Jorge Menalos and the one who calls himself Tranquilo now stand between me and untold riches, immense power.*
> *Tomorrow at 10 A.M.—and I still marvel that Tranquilo has revealed this knowledge to me—Menalos will be gone, along with the Russians who would only usurp power. Tomorrow at 10 A.M., the bomb will go off and the new guard will step forward. At that time I will know the name of Tranquilo and I shall dispatch him and—*

The chugging sound of a distant motor caught Damorcito's attention. He stopped writing and looked up at the silk-draped window to the west. He recognized that sound.

The helicopter was coming for him. He looked at the diamond-encrusted watch on his pink wrist. It wasn't time for the helicopter. It was to come just after the bomb went off, to take him to the Governor's Mansion to meet with Tranquilo.

Instinct made Damorcito wary. He locked the ledger in his wall safe and rushed to the window to part the silk draperies.

It was a helicopter, but not the one that was to come for him tomorrow morning. The helicopter now fluttering down from the crest of the mountain was a monster, a gunship.

Damorcito knew a moment of fear, of deep awareness, even before he saw the great tongue of flame leap from the belly of the gunship.

A rocket.

He leaped back from the window, fully expecting the rocket to explode harmlessly against the side of the stone villa.

The rocket didn't explode harmlessly. It soared through the window, past the fear-filled, quivering body of Jesus Damorcito, and exploded against the opposite wall of the study.

Damorcito's scream was drowned out by the thunderous roar of the rocket's payload. The room full of his precious riches suddenly exploded in flame. From outside, Damorcito could hear the sounds of other rockets, then of automatic weapons. His guards were fighting back.

But it was too late for Damorcito. The fire had reached him in the twinkling of an eye, setting him afire. He screamed and ran straight into even larger flames.

The building shook with the concussive shock of a tremendous explosion as a fire bomb was dropped from the Cobra gunship to the roof of the villa.

Jesus Damorcito did not feel the explosion. He was screaming out the last of his breath as flames engulfed his body. When he tried to take back his breath, it was full of heat and fire and death.

TEN

At the precise moment the first rocket was hurled through the window of Jesus Damorcito's study, incinerating the little would-be dictator, the jeep bearing Nick Carter and Irena Balleta was nearing the villa's gate.

The attack puzzled Carter. If the same enemy who had ordered the mortar attack on Maria Escobar's ranch had ordered the attack on Damorcito's villa, it had to be for different reasons.

The previous attack had been designed to kill Carter— and possibly Irena.

This attack, now underway, was strictly for the purpose of eliminating Jesus Damorcito.

Why?

To get the answer to that, Carter knew he would have to halt the attack before the big Cobra helicopter ruined the place and killed the man who was touted to be the contact for fissionable materials.

"Hang on, Irena," he said. "We're going in close."

"Nick, this is suicide! Why go into that inferno?"

"Do you see those guards running around shooting at the Cobra? They have the proper weapons, but they haven't the foggiest notion of how to use them. And I have only my Luger. I need one of those rifles."

Even as he spoke, he rammed the jeep through the high iron gate at the villa's main entrance. And the fire bombs continued to fall on the villa's roof.

Machine gun fire from the helicopter was sweeping the courtyard where the guards stood foolishly in the open, firing wildly into the darkening sky.

Carter saw two guards drop, both cut in two by the withering machine gun fire from above. Fifty calibers, Carter guessed. Wicked, lethal, devastating. But not overly accurate. The gunner had lucked out killing the two guards; quantity had made up for quality.

The quantity of copper-sheathed bullets sweeping the courtyard and the villa was stupendous. Carter waited for the gunner to move his firing arc to the opposite side of the courtyard before slamming on the brakes and hopping out.

"Get under the jeep!" he shouted back to Irena. "Get some cover!"

He didn't watch to see if she obeyed. He ran to the first dead guard and snatched up his rifle, an AK-47. He snared a second rifle for backup and ran to a small stone building near the south wall. It was a guard shack.

Carter set up his position in the doorway. He tracked the Cobra, took dead aim on the fuel tanks, then squeezed the trigger.

A barrage of vicious fire spat from the muzzle of the weapon. Carter stayed on track, following the Cobra's fuel tanks as the dark machine crossed above him.

All hell broke loose just then. Fire bombs the copter had dropped on its latest sweep went off in and around the villa, blowing stone and debris out in a fiery halo.

Carter saw guards being flung into the air, screaming, tumbling end over end. He saw the jeep rise from the ground and do a full gainer in the air. Irena was under the jeep. She saw the vehicle coming down at her and scrambled to safety.

Carter was blown through the open doorway of the guard shack. His body smashed against the back wall, and he felt himself losing consciousness. His head had taken a wicked crack against the stone.

He shook off the fuzziness, then heard the encouraging sounds of an engine in trouble. He crawled from the shack and gazed off to the south.

The Cobra was dropping swiftly down the side of the mountain, the way Antonio Vortez's limousine had dropped over that cliff.

The rotor blades were still whirling, but they weren't grabbing air.

A fireball suddenly erupted from the belly of the copter. Carter's well-tracked bullets had found their target, and more. They'd punctured the fuel tanks, all right, but had also torn out a section of the copter's aerial controls. The tanks hadn't exploded from the impact of hot copper and steel, but from an electrical spark from those damaged controls.

And the copter took less time than the limousine to find Valhalla. Only a few hundred yards from the south wall, it struck an outcropping of rock. Carter watched it break apart in a second explosion of flame and flying debris.

Still puzzling over why the military chopper had no markings and why it had made its attack on the villa, Carter rushed across the courtyard to Irena.

She was cowering against a wall, scared but unhurt. The mangled jeep lay in a heap only a few feet away.

"Can you walk?"

"Of course I can walk. But where can I walk to?"

True enough. The villa was in flames. Most of its massive walls had been blown out. There was a garage beyond the villa, but it too was in flames. There was only the small sentry shack. Carter left the shaky, quivering Irena there, then made a quick recon.

Damorcito's guards were dead. Those that hadn't been riddled and split apart by fifty-caliber machine gun slugs in the courtyard had been blown to bits or burned to a crisp

in the building. Not all. Several had taken refuge in a
small woodshed behind the villa, unwilling to fight for
their rich master.

A fire bomb had made a direct hit on the woodshed.

Carter started to do a body count, using the charred
bones, became nauseous, and decided to wait for the fires
to burn themselves out.

It took two hours for the ruins to cool enough for Carter
to go inside. Several rooms of the massive estate were still
nearly intact. His hopes of finding Damorcito alive
heightened. He was convinced that the man must have
expected the attack and would have an underground shelter.

There was a shelter, well provisioned and decorated by
a master, but Jesus Damorcito was not in it.

Carter found the man by accident. In the ashes of a
first-floor room he found a charred corpse and was ready
to turn away from it when he saw something glittering in
the dark debris. Diamonds, and other gems. There was
also a huge safe, its door knocked open. From the look of
things, it appeared that the body and the safe had plunged
from an upper floor.

Carter peered into the safe and saw a metal strongbox
that was blackened by fire but otherwise undamaged. He
took a stick of unburnt wood and fished out the strongbox.
With a deft flick of Hugo, he picked the lock and popped
the lid. The contents of the box were hot but intact. Carter
worked the journal out, cleared a space on the tilting floor,
and opened the book.

There was no time to read the entire journal, even
though it was obviously the diary of a man who aspired to
great power and wealth, who had committed every possible immoral and illegal act to achieve them, and who
might possibly shed light on this chamber of horrors that
Puerto Rico had become. Carter went to the back of the
journal and scanned the recent entries.

The name Tranquilo popped up often. Damorcito obviously hated and feared Tranquilo as a superior and as a competitor.

Damorcito didn't name the man, but he made it clear that he, Damorcito, planned all along to wrench power from the secret leader. Grimly, Carter read the final entry.

"Jesus," he muttered aloud to the creaking, smoldering timbers of the ancient villa. "They're setting off the bomb *tomorrow*, not on Thursday."

Even though time had now become even more precious than he'd guessed it could be, Carter took time to leaf through the pages of the diary. There could be important clues, vital data. He found several references to Alto Primero, the mountaintop villa-lab he'd destroyed just after arriving on the island.

He was just about to close the book, when he came across mention of Alto Segundo, the second mountaintop lab. He read the words slowly.

"We established it in utmost secrecy," Damorcito wrote, "because Tranquilo had information that authorities in Washington might know the location of Alto Primero. The second laboratory, located in an old monastery called Alto Beneficio, has been renamed Alto Segundo."

Carter recalled seeing a photo of the old monastery. He'd marked it with an X, indicating that the squadron of choppers Hawk would send should check it out and take additional photos. Not far from the monastery, he remembered, was the mountain he'd marked with an O, for the squadron to set up a strike force.

So far, so good. The next step, Carter knew, was to find the location of the downtown building, the place where the atomic bomb had been taken and set to go off the following morning. He continued leafing through the journal.

There were numerous references to the downtown site, but no names, no descriptions, no signs leading to its actual location.

Then Carter found something else that troubled him.

The man named Tranquilo had been instrumental in the theft of fissionable materials from the nuclear power plant.

The man named Tranquilo was, indeed, in a high position.

The highest? Carter's mind asked.

The highest man in Puerto Rico, of course, was the governor. Carter knew the governor, as did David Hawk. His record and his ethics were unimpeachable.

Tranquilo had to be someone else, someone not as high as the governor, but damned high nevertheless. *Just who the hell could that be?* Carter wondered. *A military man?*

Perhaps.

That would be General Julio Pasquez.

It was possible, just possible. The general was in Washington attending a conference at the Pentagon, a conference arranged many months ago. If Carter's hunch was right, it was important that General Pasquez be in Puerto Rico at the time the bomb was detonated.

Because Carter knew now that he had the answer to a question he had asked that man on the mountain, that young Los Bravos guard named Santiago.

Carter had asked: "Why would the leaders kill so many of their own people to gain independence?"

An answer had been given by Irena Balleta, but it wasn't the right answer. The correct answer was that independence would *not* be given if an atomic bomb were to be set off in downtown San Juan.

The correct answer was that an instant after the bomb went off, the President would declare a state of emergency and place the island under military control.

Carter had known that from the beginning, but he hadn't made the connection between "the highest" and the military factor.

Tranquilo was not peaceful at all. He was just the opposite. He was a warmonger, a militarist who would see this whole island in flames if he couldn't rule it in his own way.

Tranquilo was the man who would be named military head of Puerto Rico once military rule were established. Or he would be the man to wrest control from the head.

Carter's mind whirled with such thoughts, at such warped twistings and turnings of a man's ambition. He had no answers any longer. He knew only that someone would set off a bomb at ten o'clock tomorrow morning— just thirteen hours away—and that he, Nick Carter, was perhaps the only man trying to stop him.

And he had no idea how to do it.

For one thing, he and Irena were stranded on this scorched mountaintop. There wasn't a workable vehicle within miles. It was a long way from Muniz Air Force Base and the man who called himself Tranquilo.

Carter had a plan, but he needed quick transportation to carry it out.

ELEVEN

"Patch me through to the squadron commander," Hawk barked into the telephone. "And step on it!"

The head of AXE sat in a room on Dupont Circle. The rear wall of the room looked like a military command post. Lights flickered on computer consoles and silent radios. Hawk, sweating and chewing on an unsavory-looking cigar butt, held a telephone to his ear. The cord to the receiver led into a computer console.

He had finally reached the President, dragging him out of a dinner meeting at the Biltmore. When the President had agreed that the special squadron could be used as backup for N3's latest sortie into the land of terror, Hawk had breathed a long sigh of relief.

He, Hawk, had already dispatched the squadron an hour earlier. He had lied to the Air Force commandant, insisting that the President had given him the authority to scramble the squadron. If the President hadn't been pried out of his meeting and if he hadn't given that authority, Hawk and all of AXE would be in very, very hot water.

But it had worked out, as Hawk knew it would. All but one thing:

The squadron commander couldn't reach N3 by radio.

The squadron, only minutes away from Puerto Rico by

air, had already completed the first part of the mission by
flying over and photographing the mountain areas Carter
had marked with Xs. Much of the squadron was billeted at
the place marked with an O, but the commander, a young
captain named Joshua Billings, was out alone trying to
raise Carter by radio.

Hawk had listened to the fruitless effort on his own
radio for ten minutes, and his patience was exhausted.
That was why he demanded to be patched through to the
squadron commander.

"Captain Billings here," the strong, firm voice crackled into the office.

"This is the commandant of control center," Hawk
said, knowing that the official-sounding but nonexistent
authority would work its magic on the military mind.
"What is your position, Captain Billings?"

The captain gave a position that Hawk checked on his
map. The squadron commander was southwest of San
Juan, in the mountains. As far as Hawk was concerned,
Carter was also in those mountains. The last report he'd
received had Carter and a woman Air Force colonel racing
hell-for-leather on another wild-goose chase, looking for
someone by the name of Jesus Damorcito.

That information had come from the office of General
Julio Pasquez at Muniz; it had to be considered authentic.

"It's important that you establish contact with our
man," Hawk told Captain Billings. "ComSat supports
your visual report that the trawler is on a heading for San
Felipe, Puerto Rico. Our man is being swayed from the
real target and is on a wild-goose chase in the mountains.
Have you tried all three frequencies given to you?"

The radio Nick Carter carried had a capability of only
three frequencies, but he could be reached or picked up
within a radius of ninety miles. Unless Carter had left
Puerto Rico altogether, he should be getting the broadcasts from Captain Billings.

"Affirmative, sir," the squadron commander replied.

"And I've been repeating the message every thirty seconds for the past half hour."

Above the voice of the captain, Hawk could hear the muttering helicopter blades. The big Bell Cobra was chewing up a lot of sky over the mountains of Puerto Rico, but still the pilot hadn't spotted the agent Hawk had referred to as "our man."

"Have you seen any vehicles that seem to be racing dangerously over mountain roads?" Hawk asked the squadron chief. If Carter was down there in a vehicle, he'd probably be driving like a man possessed. He always did.

"Negative, sir. The only unusual thing I've seen so far were some bright flashes about ten miles east."

"Bright flashes?" Hawk was already checking the map to see what lay ten miles east of the pilot's position.

"Yes, sir. Kind of like fireworks."

Hawk traced a finger over the map from a point ten miles east of the helicopter's position north to San Juan. It jibed. Yes, Carter would have to come up those mountains because they had the only really traversable road in the area. It was possible that the bright flashes—the fireworks—had come from the villa of Jesus Damorcito, the man the general's office said Carter was going to see.

"Captain, tell me something," Hawk said into the special receiver. "Could those flashes have been fire bombs?"

There was a long pause, then: "It's possible, sir. I've never been in combat, but I've seen fire bombs from a distance. Do you have reason to suspect that anyone would use fire bombs up here?"

"I have reason to believe anything and everything," Hawk said, his voice low and gravelly. "Captain, I want you to check out that area. Look for a man and a woman. The woman may be wearing an Air Force uniform. The man should be the one we're looking for."

"Will do, sir." The sound of a motor revving blared into the room, and then the captain clicked off.

"One last thing, Captain," Hawk said, renewing the connection. "If it is our man, let your own command post know and then give the man a message for me."

"Yes, sir. What's the message?"

"Tell him he's to report to General Julio Pasquez at Muniz Air Force Base. The general presumably is on his way there from Washington. I want you to fly our man there personally."

"Yes, sir. Will do."

The personnel at Muniz Air Force Base were accustomed to seeing lights in the general's office at night. The hard-bitten old soldier often worked late. They were, however, surprised to see lights there that night. The general, they knew, was in Washington.

But Colonel Emilio Sangre was not. He was in the general's office, working late, but not on military business. The sergeant had long ago gone to her quarters, and all Air Force personnel not needed for Sangre's plans had been given special leave. They were all off the base except for a few who had no money to go into San Juan. The colonel was on the telephone again.

"I don't doubt the word of your men, Jorge," Sangre snapped into the receiver, "but I just cannot believe that the man from Washington survived that mortar attack on the old lady's house. Even if he did, it's too much to accept that he made it to Damorcito's villa just as my special task force arrived. And then you expect me to accept the fact that Carter single-handedly shot down the unmarked Cobra I provided."

"Why do you keep questioning me on that?" Menalos demanded. "I told you exactly what our man reported. He was the only survivor of the crash. He used the helicopter's radio to call my lieutenant downstairs in the radio room."

"But how could he be certain that the man was Carter?"

"I told you once. I'll tell you again. He saw a man and a woman arrive in a U.S. Navy jeep. He saw the man grab two rifles from two dead guards. He saw the man firing up at the helicopter, saw the tongues of flame. He heard the bullets hit. The copter went into a dive and a spin. What more evidence do you need to prove that it was that agent from Washington?"

The colonel sighed, blowing smoke at the receiver. "All right. I've already put out a message to the FBI telling them the general wants to see Mr. Carter on urgent business. We must convince Carter that the bomb is going to San Felipe and is not at your headquarters. A special squadron has been sent and has already spotted the trawler and the trucks. That will make the story more believable."

"And what will you do with Carter when and if he does come to the base?"

"He will be convinced, or he will be dealt with. Is there any further word on Damorcito? We must be certain that he died in the attack by the Cobra."

"As I told you, our man said the first rocket went directly into Damorcito's study. The fat man was standing in the window at the time. There is no way he could have survived."

"We must verify his death," Colonel Sangre said. "And make certain he did not leave evidence behind. I know that he kept a diary."

"He is dead," Menalos insisted. "As for any diary, the fire would have destroyed that. Personally—"

"I don't care what your personal thoughts are! *I'm* the military expert here!"

The colonel broke the connection and made a call to his flight control tower.

"Sergeant, dispatch an unmarked gunship to Trujillo Alto. The pilot is to land and verify the death of Jesus Damorcito. He is also to check for evidence that might have survived the fire. After that, he is to search the roadway for a man and a woman, on foot. They cannot have gone far. The pilot is to make certain that man and woman do not leave the mountain alive.''

The colonel hung up, slumped in his chair, and sucked listlessly on his cigar. He hadn't the strength to take a good, strong drag. He was weary.

Weary of this game that could put him at the head of the new nation of Puerto Rico.

Weary of ambitious men like Antonio Vortez and Jesus Damorcito. And, of course, Jorge Menalos.

Weary, most of all, of supermen like Nicholas Carter who refused to die in well-planned attacks, who pressed onward and upward in spite of all odds.

He just wished he had such men on his side. Well, either Carter would be on his side, through subterfuge and manipulation, or he would be on no side at all. He'd be dead.

Nick Carter and Irena Balleta were only a little way down the mountain when they heard the two helicopters. Carter recognized the engine sounds. One was a Cobra gunship, the other a small Sikorsky bubbletop. When they came into view, one streaking down from the direction of Muniz AFB, the other zooming in from the west, Carter saw that both the Cobra and the bubbletop were military but unmarked.

He sensed almost immediately that the Cobra was friendly, the other an enemy. A battle was going to take place up there, and he thought he knew why. He pulled Irena against a cliff wall.

He silently cursed himself for having lost the radio. It was obvious to him that the Cobra pilot had been trying to contact him and couldn't, and had come in for a look-see. The Sikorsky was from Muniz, but it wasn't there out of concern. It had been sent out by Tranquilo to eliminate the man from Washington.

Irena clung to Carter. She was weak and trembling even

though they had come only a few hundred yards from the ruined villa. Once, Carter had tried a shortcut to avoid a switchback in the road, but the jungle was too thick. They'd had to climb back to the road.

Even Carter was getting tired. But the sight of the Air Force gunship stirred adrenaline. The Killmaster and the colonel watched the two flying machines circle each other for advantage.

The Cobra had a considerable edge with its long-range firepower. The bubbletop had no effective weapon—at best a sniper, riding shotgun.

Carter could picture the radio communications taking place up there. The Air Force pilot would be trying to identify the bubbletop, and the bubbletop's pilot would be surprised to see a stateside gunship up here in the mountains of Puerto Rico.

Carter knew the answers to the questions that both pilots might be pondering.

The unmarked Cobra that had destroyed Damorcito's villa had failed in the second phase of its two-pronged mission, which was to kill the man from Washington and perhaps Colonel Balleta as well. Tranquilo had sent out the bubbletop to complete the mission, and the Air Force Cobra no doubt contained the commander of the squadron that was to back up Nick Carter. He had come, Carter mused, just in time.

The battle was about to begin. The distinctive roar of a revving engine came to his ears as the bubbletop made a wide, circling reconnaissance around the big Cobra. Carter looked up and saw that a long black object protruded from an opening in the bubbletop. It was, he suspected, a high-powered rifle.

The people in the bubbletop were going to fire while the pilot of the Cobra was still trying to get answers to questions. First fire would be a distinct advantage, Carter knew. He also knew, from the way the big Cobra moved in the sky, that the pilot was neither experienced in battle nor sufficiently wary of his enemy.

Hell, the pilot probably hasn't pegged the bubbletop yet as an enemy, Carter thought.

The high-powered rifle boomed in the night sky. The sniper was using tracer bullets, and Carter and Irena watched the fiery arc as the missile closed the distance and shot past the Cobra. The Cobra dropped like a rock, though, as the pilot learned in a hurry that he was in danger.

It was the Cobra pilot's turn to fire. He unleashed a rocket, and the fiery projectile fairly leaped from the belly of the gunship.

And it missed.

Carter watched the rocket speed past the bubbletop and make a slow, descending arc beyond the dark mountaintop. Seconds later, Carter and Irena heard the hollow boom echo through the hills and valleys as the shell exploded into a hillside.

The Sikorsky now had the advantage. The green Cobra pilot had sped past it, expecting his rocket to have blasted it to bits by now. The bubbletop came up in an expert, screaming climb and held onto the Cobra's tail while the sniper worked into position.

The booming rifle ripped through the humid air. In time, the sniper would work the tracers down into the Cobra's path. The Cobra pilot was inexperienced but hardly stupid. Carter grinned as the big gunship, having gauged the path of the tracers, made a neat sidestep maneuver just before the rifle bullets met his path.

And then the Cobra again dropped suddenly, falling almost helter-skelter toward the dark mountain. Carter heard the engine rev and scream as the gunship came within a few feet of the jungle growth, then began a nose-up climb directly into the flight path of the now wavering Sikorsky.

The pilot cut loose once with the 20mm. Six yards of

flame burst from the nose of the Cobra. Through the flame ripped the lethal shell, a dark and deadly missile that sped unerringly toward a point ahead of the onrushing bubbletop.

The explosion was bright and gaudy, decorating the black sky with a display that would pale the most extravagant Fourth of July starburst. The sound came an instant later, roaring and rumbling and echoing up and down the mountains and valleys. Irena screamed. Carter held her close. Pieces of aircraft and fragments of the 20mm shell rained on them. Carter felt something wet hit him, and he knew it was a part of what had recently been a human being. He hit the dirt, pulling the lady with him.

When the hail of debris stopped, there was only the chugging sound of the big Cobra, zinging back and forth over the dark hills. The pilot was obviously looking for something.

Carter's face was close to Irena's. She kissed him hard. He let the kiss last five seconds, not wanting it to end at all. Finally, he pulled away.

"Stay here, Irena," he said. "The man in the Cobra came to look for us. I've got to give him a signal."

He ran to the center of the road, shucking his jacket and shirt as he went. He piled them in the road. He'd have given his right arm for a flare pistol, but then he'd also have given practically any part of him for the radio he'd lost. However, he'd have to make do with what he had and keep his more vital parts.

Carter realized that the shirt and jacket would make only a puny, short-lived fire for the pilot to see. He stepped out of his trousers and added them to the pile. Irena didn't object when he insisted that she contribute her skirt and the blouse that Maria Escobar had given her.

And he didn't bother to avert his eyes from her lovely nakedness as she stood clad only in panties and shoes. He

looked away reluctantly to touch his lighter to the pile of
clothing. He watched it smoke, smolder, and then burst
into flame.

The timing had been perfect. The Cobra pilot was just
about to leave the area to search elsewhere when the fire
burned its brightest. The pilot saw the flames and went
into idle, hovering above it. He flipped on his landing
lights.

The pilot whistled, and his whistle was heard in
Washington by a man named Hawk who was monitoring
the squadron chief's radio. Hawk, who had reinstated the
direct patch during the dogfight with the Sikorsky, broke
in:

"What's the whistle for, Captain Billings?"

"Sorry, sir," the pilot said. "There are two people on
the road below. They're about as naked as people can get.
The woman is something to see, especially from this view
and in these bright landing lights."

"Get on with it!" Hawk barked.

Carter watched the Cobra do a slow flyover and land at
a wide switchback twenty yards down the hill. The engine
died, the rotor blades whined more slowly, and the right
side door opened. The Air Force captain stood in the open
hatchway, grinning as Nick Carter and the woman ran to
the copter.

"If I were a publisher," Captain Billings said as he and
Carter helped Irena into the gunship, "I'd pay a hundred
dollars a word for the story of what's been going on up
here."

Carter closed the door and dropped the safety latch.

"I'll bet you would," he snapped. "But right now,
let's get the hell off this mountain!"

"Sure thing. You'll find some fatigues in my duffel bag
back there. I don't think the general would appreciate this
scene the way I'm appreciating it."

"The general? General who?"

"Pasquez."

"What about him?" Carter felt an uncomfortable pinch somewhere in the area that usually warned him of danger.

"He wants to see you," the captain said as he kicked over the engine and started the blades whirring again. "I'm to take you there."

The pilot didn't see the look of surprise on Carter's face. He was too busy watching Irena put on a fatigue jacket and button it up over those voluptuous breasts.

But Carter couldn't have been more surprised if the pilot had said that the President himself wanted to see him. He waited until the big ship was airborne, then he asked a question that, to him, was the most obvious question to ask.

"You're taking us to Washington?"

The pilot tore his eyes away from Irena and gawked at Carter. "No, sir. I'm taking you to Muniz Air Force Base. Where do you think the general is?"

"I'm beginning to wonder," Carter said with a sigh. He settled into the comfortable copilot's seat and pondered this latest development and what it meant.

Again, there were a lot of questions but few answers.

TWELVE

A minute after takeoff, Nick Carter looked back to see Irena Balleta asleep on the floor of the helicopter. He, too, was exhausted. It had been more than forty hours since he had slept, almost twenty-four since he had stepped off the Coast Guard cutter with his warpack and the big Weatherby Mark V. He envied Irena her sleep.

Ahead, he knew, was more trouble than he cared to handle. It was incredible that the general was back from Washington, yet it fit. The general could easily be the man who called himself Tranquilo. Had he deliberately made himself absent from the island while the power struggle took place?

And it had been a struggle. First, Antonio Vortez was killed. Carter had done the killing, but he was convinced that it had been a calculated risk on the part of those in power. If Carter had been the one to die, Vortez would have met death in another way. Then had come Jesus Damorcito. That had been pure extermination; there was no other word for it.

Who would be next? Perhaps Jorge Menalos—unless the nuclear physicist were Tranquilo. Perhaps General Pasquez? Who would win the lottery of death that seemed to be the game of the day in Puerto Rico? And who would lose? It could very well be one Nick Carter.

"You have messages, sir," the pilot said, breaking Carter from his reverie. "Would you like them now?"

"Sure. Shoot."

Captain Billings coughed into his hand, then cleared his throat like a tenor about to perform at the Met. "First off, sir," he said tentatively, "I'm to relate to you that everyone from the Pentagon to the State Department is convinced that you have been on, well, sir, a wrong track."

"What do they consider the right track?"

"I can confirm part of that, sir," the pilot said. "I flew—"

"Let's knock off this 'sir' stuff, okay? My name's Nick. What's yours?"

"Josh, sir."

"Okay, Josh, sir, continue with the messages."

"Yes, si—sure. I flew a course between Cuba and here, and I can verify the ComSat report that a Cuban trawler is on a heading for San Felipe. According to speed and winds, it will arrive at port at a little after four in the morning."

"All right." Carter thought of the trawler and of its real purpose, recalling a line from Damorcito's diary "Tomorrow at 10 A.M. . . . Menalos will be gone, along with the Russians who would only usurp power." Were there Soviets on that trawler? Had they been backing this gambit all along, planning to step in at the final moment and grasp power from those who planned it? And was Tranquilo planning all along to eliminate the Russians before they could exact their pound of flesh? He turned to the pilot. "Go on, Josh. You confirm the trawler. What else?"

"One of my pilots checked out the trucks that left Alto Primero at dawn and holed up in a little mountain town halfway to the southern coast. The trucks left a garage just after dark and are now on their way to San Felipe. My man had special equipment aboard. He confirms that the trucks—or one of them, at least—is carrying something very hot.''

"You mean hot as in radioactive?''

"Yes, sir. I mean Nick.''

"It could be the bomb,'' Carter said with a weary sigh. "I could be wrong, as the Pentagon and State think. That guy Santiago could have lied through his teeth to set me on the wrong track. Or . . .''

"Or what?'' the pilot asked when Carter did not continue.

"Or the trawler and the trucks are decoys. The radiation could come from raw plutonium prepared for use at a second laboratory. There is a second laboratory, isn't there? I mean, you did check out the spots I suggested?''

"We checked them. The number three spot, twelve miles northwest of Alto Primero—do you remember it?''

"I remember.'' But Carter barely did, however. He had seen the photos only briefly before he'd sent them on to Washington. Was it only that morning? Carter thought. It seemed like years.

"It's an old monastery called Alto Beneficio,'' Captain Billings said. "One of my pilots saw guard dogs, and I went for a personal look-see. There is a minefield on the western approach, but the wall is clear, as it was at Alto Primero.''

Carter moaned, thinking of another high wall to scale. "Anything else?'' he asked the young squadron commander.

"Yes. Those names you sent to Washington? They've been checked by every computer the government has. Everyone is clean. The girl back there''—he threw a quick grin in Irena's direction—"well, she's one hell of an officer. She's won every honor the Air Force has to give.''

"And a few that you'd like to confer, I suppose?'' Carter asked, returning the grin.

"Well, she sure is gorgeous . . .''

"I know. And what you tell me is good news. What about the one called Tranquilo? Did the computers spit anything out on him?

"No. Nothing at all."

Okay. So the big colonel, Emilio Sangre, was clean. So were the general and Antonio Vortez and Jorge Menalos. What did it mean? Only that none of them had ever been officially reprimanded or arrested. It didn't mean they were innocent of what was happening now.

"Anything else?" Carter asked the pilot.

"Just one thing. A man from control center has been patching in from time to time. He seems to be quite concerned about you. Sir, I checked all my organizational charts, and I can't even find an outfit called 'control center.' Do you know anything about it?"

Carter grinned. He could see Hawk monitoring the pilot's radio broadcasts and getting worried when Carter didn't respond to the pilot's calls. Hawk couldn't know that his agent had lost the special radio. And, yes, he'd be the kind to patch in and use a hokey authority like "control center." He looked somberly at the pilot.

"I haven't the faintest idea what it is," he said.

"Oh," Josh Billings said, looking pensive. "I was sure you would."

Carter stared ahead at the dark night, then at the jungle moving swiftly past below. The big Cobra engine throbbed hypnotically, but Carter's thoughts were far from calm. They were troubled, uncertain. The plan that he'd toyed with before was no clearer in his mind. There were too many uncertainties.

A few things were clear, though—at least to him. One, the bomb was not on a truck heading for San Felipe; it was at a downtown building as the dying Santiago had told him. Two, the trawler was not coming to pick up the trucks and the bomb; it was delivering a bunch of Russians who had helped Tranquilo but who were now to be eliminated. Three, the bomb was going to be detonated at ten o'clock tomorrow morning, not at eleven on Thursday. Four, the man called Tranquilo and the nuclear physicist named Jorge Menalos were the only two important leaders left; the others had been systematically terminated. And five, the man called Tranquilo was almost certainly a military man, perhaps even General Pasquez himself.

Nick Carter was heading for the island's chief military base to be the guest of General Pasquez. Why?

Carter toyed with the idea of refusing to go to Muniz Air Force Base. He was, he suspected, flying into some kind of trap. All other efforts to kill or dissuade him had failed. Was he being summoned to the lion's den to be the main course of a very large dinner? It would be easy to squirm out of the invitation. He had only to put Wilhelmina's muzzle to this young Air Force captain's temple and order him to fly somewhere else. Anywhere.

But a plan began to take shape. It required Carter to put his flesh on the tip of a high stake as bait for the people who planned—and planned all along—to kill him. Bait, he knew, was not necessarily a dinner item. Sometimes, bait escaped. He had been bait many times and had escaped uneaten. He just hoped he hadn't used up all his luck in that particular area.

"Josh," he said as he saw the lights of San Juan appearing in the distance, "I want you to do me a favor."

"Sure, Nick. What is it?"

"You still have the attack force bivouacked up on the mountain I suggested?"

"Sure do."

"Keep it there. I want you to join your other pilots after you drop me off at Muniz but I want you to return at precisely midnight. That's two hours and thirty-six minutes from now. If I'm not out on the helipad to meet you, consider me dead. I want you and your attack force to hit Alto Beneficio with everything you've got. The least I can do is stall them off on the building of future bombs."

"Sir—Nick, are you certain you want us to hit that lab?

I mean, it could scatter radiation all over the area if they have plutonium up there.''

"They don't have it up there," Carter said flatly. "They have it in the trucks. Once you report what's happened to me, I'm sure those trucks will be picked up and the plutonium returned to whatever monster hole it came from. I want you to promise me, though, that you'll destroy Alto Beneficio, otherwise known as Alto Segundo. Don't even ask permission from your commanding officer.''

"I'll do it. You can count on it." There was a frog in the captain's voice, and Carter was afraid he'd go on and say something about not letting the man from Washington die in vain, but the young man was silent.

And the big Bell Cobra moved noisily through the night, heading for Muniz and whatever fate awaited Killmaster N3. Above all else, Carter wanted sleep—just a few hours, not an eternity of it.

Yet an eternity it could be.

Although Colonel Sangre had a plush apartment in downtown San Juan, a tobacco ranch in the Arecibo region, and a villa on the side of Cerro de Punta, Puerto Rico's highest mountain, in the Ponce district, he was staying in his quarters at Muniz AFB.

A man of many facets, the large, eternally scowling colonel with the fat, black cigars had a wife and three children living at his tobacco ranch. He kept a few lovely women on call at his downtown apartment. But at his villa on Cerro de Punta, there were no women. Colonel Sangre went there only when he experienced religious feelings. He used the villa much as a monk would use a retreat.

He went to the villa to meditate, to pray, to reach his God in whichever way he could.

His religious feelings were deep, but they were bred of fear, not of a love for God. He firmly believed that no

matter what manner of evil he might do to his fellow men
on his climb to power and wealth, his God would forgive
him and take him into the kingdom of heaven. Or, better
yet, would spare him and make an exception to the rule
that all living things must die.

His fear stemmed from a deep-seated belief that his God
might act capriciously, might deny him his rightful re-
wards on earth and in heaven. Therefore, he prayed a lot,
hoping to keep on his God's good side. A capricious God
might forgive, but He certainly couldn't be trusted.

The colonel's monthly pilgrimages to Cerro de Punta
where, almost 4,500 feet above the jungle floor, he could
talk to his God, cajole Him, placate Him, even offer to
bribe Him, were as important to him as were the reliable
lieutenants he kept close to his quarters at Muniz AFB.

The colonel's quarters were at one end of the bachelor
officers' quarters building. They contained a meeting
room as well as a bedroom, a study, a kitchen, and a
spacious, well-appointed living room.

On the night that Nick Carter was to come to Muniz, by
his own design and at the ''general's request,'' Colonel
Sangre had excused all of the regular base officers, who
had returned to their homes in the city. The colonel's
special lieutenants, most of them armed goons given
commissions they didn't deserve, occupied the BOQ
space in the colonel's wing.

One room in the center of the wing lay vacant.

It was the room reserved for the man from Washington
to catch a few hours of sleep before the colonel's special
team, carrying machetes, swooped down for a special kill.
Los Bravos, of course, would be blamed.

''There must be no slips,'' Sangre said to the tall hulk of
a man who looked uncomfortable in his crisp blue Air
Force uniform. ''When I give the word, I want the team to
cut through the fence, make a swift kill, leave a machete
as a token, and escape the same way. I want the regular

guards to be distracted by a fire down by the VX-4 Squadron hangars. See that everything goes smoothly, Lieutenant Ospina.''

''*Sí*,'' the apelike lieutenant responded. ''Shortly before midnight, the fire will commence. Within two minutes, the gringo will be dead. Los Bravos will be blamed.''

The colonel sighed, disappointed that this empty-headed thug could only echo his own words. Yet he'd have been angry if the man hadn't been an echo. As much as he detested stupidity in others, he feared intelligence in everyone. Intelligent people asked questions, had ideas of their own, were dangerous.

Like that damned Jorge Menalos.

Colonel Sangre had needed Menalos when he had recruited him along with that milksop George Pierson those months before. Now he rued the day he'd brought in Jorge Menalos.

Sure, the man had produced, had set up two elaborate and successful laboratories that had already created a viable atomic bomb, with more coming.

But Menalos had gone further. His ambitions ruled him. He had set up his own guard contingent of trusted lieutenants, had formed a splinter group that threatened the colonel's own plans.

It had been a mistake to listen to Jorge Menalos's ideas, to let him meet with Antonio Vortez and Jesus Damorcito. The three had conspired, ultimately gaining more control over Los Bravos than the colonel had. Jorge Menalos had become even more of a thorn than had Damorcito and Vortez. But those two were gone now, thanks in part to the man from Washington.

All right. Menalos would get his at ten o'clock tomorrow morning, in just twelve hours. The colonel had set it all up. He'd insisted that the bomb be taken to San Juan Exports, the company that fronted for Antonio Vortez.

He'd let Menalos take the bomb there and wait for Thursday morning.

And the colonel had made excellent use of the helicopter pilot assigned to whisk Jorge Menalos away from San Juan Exports an hour before the presumed detonation time. The pilot had been trained in the delicate job of triggering a nuclear weapon and had set up a second triggering device. The pilot would fly off in the helicopter shortly before ten o'clock tomorrow morning, leaving Jorge Menalos high and dry with the hot bomb and no knowledge of the second triggering device, no knowledge that he had only minutes to live.

Along with Menalos would go the twenty Communist leaders coming to discuss ''strategy'' with the man called Tranquilo. That had been a stroke of genius getting the Russians to come at this time.

The trawler, out of Cuba, provided an excellent decoy to keep the Americans—and especially Nick Carter—from learning the truth until it was too late.

The holocaust would do many things for the career and ambitions of Colonel Emilio Sangre. It would eliminate the last of his competitors for the job of dictator in Puerto Rico. It would erase the debt to the Communists who had been helpful in providing tangential materials and advice on the setting up of the laboratories and the making of the bomb.

After the blast, military rule would be instated. As the ranking military officer on the island, General Julio Pasquez would head up the tribunal to enforce that rule.

Ah, the general. That had been the colonel's masterstroke of planning and arranging. His discovery two years ago that the general was in the early stages of Alzheimer's disease was the turning point. The disease, which caused premature senility, left the general befuddled and indecisive at times. More and more, he began to lean on Emilio Sangre to help him from being discovered, from being given early retirement from a brilliant career.

From a small beginning, it had been easy to usurp most of the general's powers of command. Sangre had himself appointed military attaché to the special committee that controlled weapons-grade radioactive materials from the Punta Jiguero nuclear power plant. Sangre opened the general's mail, handled his replies, and dispatched his orders. For two years, the colonel had, in effect, been the commanding officer of Muniz Air Force Base.

The risky part had come in letting General Pasquez attend the Pentagon conference. Sangre had sent along a trusted lieutenant to watch over the general, but it was possible that another officer might detect the problem. But the risk was necessary. Sangre needed General Pasquez out of Puerto Rico at the time of the blast, if only to remove him from suspicion. And he needed full control of the general's office and the base to win his power struggle against the others.

Once the general was returned to Muniz as head of the military tribunal effecting martial law on the island, Sangre would truly be the man in control. In time, he would become the one and only leader; he would eliminate General Julio Pasquez when it was no longer possible to uproot the colonel's military control over Puerto Rico.

Everything required delicate planning and a firm hand. The only remaining block was the man from Washington.

The colonel had been furious when he'd received the report from his man in the control tower that something bad had happened up in the mountains within the hour.

"We lost contact with the men in the Sikorsky," the air traffic controller had reported. "Our radar men report that there were *two* aircraft in the area for a time. One disappeared at the moment we lost contact."

"Have you identified the second aircraft?" the colonel demanded.

"No, sir."

"Then do it! Report to me as soon as you have done it."

The telephone rang as though he had willed it to do so. It was the man in the control tower. His man.

"Stateside Bell Cobra is approaching the base, Colonel Sangre," the man said. "The pilot requests landing approval."

"Who is it?"

"A Captain Josh Billings. He has the man named Nick Carter with him. Also Colonel Irena Balleta."

"Give approval," the colonel said, smiling broadly and gazing at the window where the landing lights of the Cobra were already spreading little stars of light across the glass.

The last stumbling block, the colonel mused as he hung up the telephone, *has just presented itself for extermination.*

THIRTEEN

The big Cobra set down shortly before ten on the helipad near the Muniz headquarters building. Carter peered through the Plexiglas at the small group of airmen and officers on the lighted tarmac. He saw Colonel Sangre looking like a uniformed gorilla and scowling at the helicopter as though he wanted to tear it to shreds with his bare hands. Carter filed the image away with the swift, sickening thought that the colonel could probably do just that if the mood struck him.

"Thanks for the taxi ride, Josh," he said to the young captain.

Captain Billings was staring at the tough-looking reception committee. "Sir, are you sure you want me to leave you here? Those guys look more like hooligans than Air Force personnel."

"They probably are hooligans," Carter said with a smile. "But then, I'm not without hooligan tendencies myself. See you at midnight, Josh."

"Is you have any trouble before then," the squadron commander said, handing a small black box to Carter, "use this."

It was another radio device, a directional transmitter.

Once activated, it would emit a signal for Captain Billings to come immediately.

"I'll hope not to use it and try not to lose it," Carter said, fairly singing the rhyming sentence. "Over and out."

With a flash of a grin below troubled eyes, Carter went aft, woke up Irena, and stepped with her into the glaring lights surrounding the helipad. Colonel Sangre stepped forward as a fuel truck rumbled up to the Cobra.

"Good evening, Mr. Carter," the colonel said, giving an uncharacteristic smile and extending his hand. "The general has been called to the Governor's Mansion for a couple of hours. He thought, since you have not rested since arriving in Puerto Rico, that you might relish a short nap."

"He's been reading my mind," Carter said. "A few things first, though. Colonel Balleta needs to visit your sick bay—I'm sure she knows where it is. And I'd like a few words with you alone."

"Certainly. Lieutenant, assist Colonel Balleta to the dispensary. This way, Mr. Carter."

Colonel Sangre chose the general's quarters for the meeting with the man from Washington. Carter noticed immediately that the place seemed unused, at least in recent days. A thin layer of dust covered the tables and knick-knacks and war souvenirs of the general. The colonel served brandy—Courvoisier—and sat opposite Carter in a plush velvet chair in the general's study.

"I don't buy the story that the bomb is en route to San Felipe to be picked up by a trawler," Carter began, getting right to the point.

The colonel sipped his brandy and studied the brown-eyed man across from him. He saw intelligence, yes, but he didn't fear it. The man was on the right track, but he was too late.

"I see. Yet your own pilot, the captain who brought you here, has confirmed that the trawler is on a course for

San Felipe and that the trucks are also heading there.''

Carter shrugged and took a sip of his brandy. He wondered if it were drugged and decided that the colonel or the general—if the general were indeed in San Juan—would not be quite so obvious.

''It really doesn't matter,'' he said tiredly. ''The Coast Guard has a bead on the trawler, and ComSat and some special forces are tracking the trucks. As for the bomb, I believe it's stashed somewhere in downtown San Juan. I'll find it. After all, I still have''—he looked at his watch—''almost thirty-six hours, right?''

Carter watched the colonel's eyes. Did he see a sparkle of glee there, a self-satisfied glimmer? Did the colonel buy the idea that the man from Washington had been fooled, as Menalos apparently was being fooled? Or was the colonel totally innocent? Should Carter save his baiting tactics for the general? What the hell—he was here, so why not check the colonel out?

''I see,'' the colonel said again. ''So you will continue your search tomorrow? You will require the services of Colonel Balleta, I presume.''

''Of course. But there's something else I have to do first.'' He stopped, waiting for the colonel to absorb that news and to respond to it.

''And what might that be, Mr. Carter?''

''At dawn,'' Carter said, really watching the giant's eyes now, ''a special attack force led by me will assault and destroy a nuclear bomb laboratory and manufacturing facility known as Alto Segundo.''

There it was, the whole plan, laid out for the enemy to digest and respond to.

The colonel was either innocent or more shrewd than Carter had guessed. The man's face was a blank, his eyes revealing nothing whatsoever.

''I wasn't aware that a second laboratory existed,'' he said. ''Are you certain of your facts? You could be destroying an innocent villa, you know.''

"I never said it was in a villa," Carter said. "I guess that's a logical guess on your part, though, since Alto Primero was in a villa. And yes, there is a second lab and I'm sure of my facts. It's located in an old monastery named Alto Beneficio."

"Might I ask where you are obtaining all this information?" the colonel said. He stubbed out his cigar and took another sip of brandy. Carter noticed that his large, well-manicured fingers trembled slightly on the snifter.

"Remember the aerial recon photos I picked up on my first visit here?" he asked. "I had my backup people do some flyovers. We have solid confirmation on Alto Beneficio." He decided to hold back the data he had gleaned from Damorcito's diary, although the temptation to beard the lion in his den was high. "At midnight, Captain Billings will return here for me. He'll fly me to the attack force bivouac in the mountains, and we'll plan our hit on the second lab. Beyond that, Colonel, I don't think I should tell you anything."

"You've told me quite enough," the colonel said, leaning back in his chair, seeming to relax considerably. The bait, Carter knew, had been taken. It was now the colonel's move—or the general's. "There is one problem," the colonel continued.

"Yes?"

"The general won't return until after midnight. He insists that you be here on his return."

"Do you know what he wants?"

"I haven't the slightest idea."

"It must be damned important," Carter said, "if he wouldn't tell his senior aide about it. Well, if he gets back before the gunship arrives, we'll have our talk. Otherwise, it will have to wait until after the raid on Alto Segundo. Meanwhile, I'd like that nap you promised."

"Certainly." The colonel got up and went to the general's big desk. He pressed a button. "Lieutenant Ospina will come to show you to your quarters. One more ques-

tion, Mr. Carter. If Captain Billings returns and you are
not ready to depart, or if the general should have reason to
forbid you to carry out this raid on what you call Alto
Segundo, what will happen?''

"Captain Billings himself will lead the raid. No matter
what, Alto Segundo will be blasted to hell. Those orders
supercede anything the general might have to say.''

The colonel fiddled with an unlit cigar and a gold
lighter. His fingers trembled more noticeably. Carter decided to go for broke.

"Just to make certain there's no interference,'' Carter
said, "I am now using authority granted me in
Washington to ground all your aircraft until my raid is
completed. Nothing short of an enemy attack can get your
planes off the ground, Colonel Sangre.''

He watched the giant deflate a little. Carter knew he had
won a major point. He also knew that the colonel or his
general had no choice now but to try to kill him before
midnight, and then try to find Captain Billings and his
strike force before it could complete its mission. *All hell is
about to break loose in Puerto Rico—but better tonight
than at ten o'clock tomorrow,* Carter thought.

"Well, then,'' the colonel said, smiling and looking at
his wristwatch, "it would seem that there is nothing the
general or I can do but stand and wait. I wish you good
luck on your raid, Mr. Carter. Ah, Lieutenant Ospina is
here to show you to your room. Sleep well.''

As Carter left with the hulking lieutenant, he noticed
that the colonel's hands were no longer trembling and that
the smile on the big man's face seemed to stem from some
inner joy.

Carter knew that he had placed his bait in just the right
trap.

When the silent lieutenant left Carter at the door of his
quarters, the Killmaster slipped inside and made a quick
check. No bug, no booby traps. He took a water glass
from the bathroom and balanced it on top of the doorknob.

Then he laid out his weapons. He tucked Wilhelmina under his pillow but left Hugo strapped to his forearm where a mere tensing of certain muscles would slide the stiletto into his hand. Pierre, the tiny gas bomb, was placed on the night table. He would use it only if he planned to leap through the window, which wasn't totally out of the realm of possibility.

As he put out the light and lay back in the narrow bed, smoking a cigarette, he wondered about Irena. Was it possible that she was a part of the elaborate scheme to take over Puerto Rico by terrorism and military rule and betrayal and assassination? Had she been deliverately assigned to him to keep him from gumming up the works for the man called Tranquilo?

It was just possible that she had set the trap for him at El Palacio and had somehow aided Antonio Vortez in catching up to them on the mountain road. The outcome wasn't what the culprits expected, so there was another attempt at the Escobar farm. In that attack, Irena's life was as much on the line as his. The same applied at the villa of Jesus Damorcito.

All things considered, Carter hadn't decided whether Irena was or was not involved. She was beautiful, of course, and she was passionate and willing in bed. But so, he imagined, was Mata Hari.

He couldn't make up his mind about Irena, except that he liked her and wanted her along on the upcoming raid on Alto Segundo. He would have to make the time to fetch her from her own quarters.

His mind drifted in and out of sleep, a kind of combat sleep that never let him completely lose consciousness. He couldn't afford that kind of luxury, not tonight.

FOURTEEN

There were three of them. They crossed from the enlisted men's barracks, moved in shadows, then sprinted catty-corner across the lighted compound, past the helipad.

Each of the men wore jungle-camouflage khakis. Each carried a Luger. The man leading the trio carried a decorative machete in his belt.

The main door to the BOQ was unlocked. The first man opened and held it as the others dashed through. The man went inside and closed the door.

Slowly, the three men made their way up the steps and into the lighted main corridor. They paused, as though listening for sounds of human activity, then moved along stealthily. The only sound was of the machete blade slapping gently against the leader's thigh.

At an intersection of the main corridor, the men paused again, waiting and listening. The leader made a turn to the left. The others followed.

The leader stopped at the door, then put his hand on the knob. With his free hand, he directed his two men to take up posts on either side of the door. When they were in place, guns drawn, the leader took a small strip of plastic from his pocket and inserted it between the door and the jamb.

There was a distinctive click. The leader grinned, replaced the plastic strip in his pocket, and took out his Luger. He looked at his watch, his lips moving as he counted off seconds.

The sound of a distant siren whined in the corridor. The diversionary fire had been started. The leader nodded to each of his two men and slowly turned the knob.

The sound of breaking glass was like a small bomb in the room. Nick Carter responded to it immediately.

The glass tumbler he'd taken from the bathroom and balanced on top of the doorknob had crashed to the tile floor.

Even as the door swung open and light streamed into the room, Carter was already in a far corner. The sound had awakened more than his brain.

Deep, primordial instincts had been jolted into action. His hand had gripped the butt of his beloved Luger, and his feet and shoulders had heaved his body in a twisting motion from the bed. In a planned reflex action, Carter had thrown his blanket directly toward the door.

The leader, already confused by the startling sound of the breaking glass, ran smack into the blanket and found himself blinded by the clinging cloth.

Carter aimed at the bobbing, blanket-covered head and squeezed off one round. The explosion roared in the room. The 9mm slug pierced the blanket and plunged onward through skin, skull, and brains.

A hole the size of a lemon appeared in the back of the rounded part of the blanket. Through that hole gushed a spray of red and gray fragments of human bone and tissue.

It was this bloody shower that met the second man as he dashed into the room, firing his Luger in the general direction of the bed. The man cursed, pausing to wipe his leader's remains from his face.

Carter squeezed off another shot. The hot pellet went

slightly wide. Instead of catching the man in the head, it
hit low and to the right, severing the jugular vein in the
man's neck.

A virtual cloudburst of blood met the third man. Carter
fired twice through the sheet of blood. This time, the aim
was accurate. The bullet nailed the last assassin through
his right eye.

Barely three seconds had transpired between the firing of the first booming shot and the last. The leader had
just crashed into the empty bed and was falling to the floor
as the following two men piled on top of him.

There were no death throes. All three were dead as soon
as they hit the floor, a neat pile of lifeless bodies and one
fancy machete.

Carter, still crouched in the corner with the smoking
Wilhelmina, surveyed the scene. His eyes shot to the open
doorway, then to the shattered glass on the floor.

Sounds of running footsteps thundered in the corridor.
Through that thunder came the whine of a siren. Carter
knew why. A diversionary fire.

He lunged forward, found the shaft of the machete, and
yanked. The wide, sharp blade came clear of the men's
bodies with a trace of blood on its design. Carter swung
his left arm back and waited.

The first man through the doorway was dressed in an
Air Force uniform and had an MP band on his right arm.
He carried a .45 automatic.

Carter swung hard. The blade caught the phony MP in
the throat and nearly took off the man's head. The
Killmaster dropped the machete on the growing pile of
bodies, stepped into the doorway, and faced three other
men in uniform, also wearing MP armbands.

Convenient, Carter thought. *Very convenient. The MPs
show up within seconds of the attack*. Why? To protect the
man from Washington? Or to make certain the attack
didn't fail?

But Carter had no time for guessing games. The AXE

agent had already given a name to the game when he'd killed the first MP.

Now he squeezed the trigger of his Luger and moved the weapon fractions of an inch from left to right as the muzzle bucked and spat and barked in the narrow corridor.

The spray of bullets sent the three new MPs sprawling in every conceivable manner of grotesque gyrations. Helmets flew through the air and landed with loud clanking sounds on the tile floor.

The first man did a complete pirouette, clutching his throat, blood gushing from his fingers and from his open mouth. The second man did a half gainer backward, his .45 slipping from his hand and scuttling across the floor, sliding between Carter's spread legs. The third man doubled over like a drunk vomiting, then vomited blood.

Carter was certain now. Colonel Emilio Sangre was Tranquilo. He had sent these men. If he had stopped with the Los Bravos killers, Carter might still have been guessing. But the phony MPs convinced him.

Almost.

To erase all doubt, he went through the pockets of the MPs. None had identification.

Now he was totally convinced.

Sounds were coming from other quarters up and down the corridor. The fight had taken so little time that most of the officers, who hadn't been considered necessary to the kill plan, were just getting out of bed and stumbling around to turn on lights.

Carter used that time to his advantage. He snatched up Pierre and the fatigues Billings had given him, then dashed down to the main corridor. He knew the way to General Pasquez's suite. The colonel would be there, awaiting news of the death of the man from Washington.

Carter would give him the news personally.

As he was turning into the main corridor, he heard movement behind him. Two officers in pajamas stood in the smaller hallway, .45 automatics in hand. Carter let fly with the remaining rounds in the Luger.

The first bullet caught its victim in the temple, making a dark hole in the right rear of the man's skull. The next two bullets plunged into the second officer's chest and sent the man scudding backward, dying on the way down.

Carter jammed a new clip into Wilhelmina and ran all the way to the general's suite, encountering no further interference. The plan had gone haywire. A simple killing, one that should have left them all sleeping, had suddenly erupted into a war in the BOQ. But not even the colonel's most loyal subjects wanted exposure to that war.

The colonel had promised them an easy, bloodless coup. Nick Carter was making it difficult, and bloodier than hell.

The officers cowed in their rooms, awaiting the outcome, each no doubt concocting a story to explain his noninvolvement. Meanwhile, Nick Carter had a clear road to the colonel.

He didn't bother knocking. He raised his bare foot and crashed it into the door, right beside the knob. A dim light burned in the foyer. Carter went in, trying to decide which door led to the general's bedroom.

A door on his left opened. Carter crouched, ready to fire.

The towering, apelike lieutenant, the man who had taken Carter to his room, flew out at him. There was no time to raise the Luger and fire. Only time to kick.

Carter's bare foot caught the charging man in the throat. Such a kick would have instantly strangled an ordinary man. Not the lieutenant.

The hooligan-soldier was accustomed to every kind of body punch and kick. He'd been wounded a dozen times with a dozen kinds of weapons. His whole body, brain included, was one enormous callous, one huge patch of scar tissue that felt no pain and was very nearly immune to damage.

So instead of crushing the man's windpipe with that hard kick to the throat, Carter practically sprained his ankle.

Even as Carter was falling backward after the karate kick to the lieutenant's throat, he was spinning around, getting the Luger in position to let bullets do his fighting.

Lieutenant Ospina swung a club of a fist so swiftly that Carter didn't see it before it caught him in the temple. Multicolored lights went off in his head. He felt his feet slipping from beneath him, felt consciousness leaving. He felt Wilhelmina slip from his hand.

He got a firm grip on his mind and body. He dug his toes into the general's expensive carpet, pulled himself forward, and caught the big lieutenant in the solar plexus with his head. The blow nearly broke Nick Carter's neck. The lieutenant hardly moved a muscle.

Except to bring both hands, clenched, high in the air and start down with what would have been a blow to break the back of a buffalo.

Carter made up with speed what he lacked in brute strength against this powerful enemy. He'd fought powerful, unfeeling thugs before. Once again, it was the irresistible force meeting the immovable object.

But this immovable object had to have a weak spot. All things human did. It was up to Carter to find it and exploit it.

He backed off in a feint, backing all the way to the opposite wall of the foyer. And the giant of a man moved inexorably forward.

Carter studied the huge, sweating body in the silk pajamas. There had to be a weak spot. There *had* to be. And Carter had only a fraction of a second to find it.

There are two highly sensitive and vulnerable areas on the human body: the eyes and the genitals. Each is easy to get at, but only if the adversary is taken by surprise. In a standoff, the enemy knows his own weaknesses and sets up automatic and subconscious defenses for them.

Carter had little chance of getting at the lieutenant's eyes or crotch. If he tried, he'd most certainly lose the arm or leg with which he tried.

In that fraction of a second, he decided on one of the most dangerous ploys of his long career. He would let himself be taken, but on his own terms.

He leaped high into the air, his arms upraised, his entire body vulnerable to a killing blow. But he hadn't figured the lieutenant for a puncher. He'd figured him for a crusher. And he was right.

The big ape caught Carter in midair. His arms encircled Carter's midsection. Carter felt hard knuckles gouging into his spine as the man tried for a quick jerk to snap that spine.

Carter didn't resist the jerk. He let the knuckles come, let his body become pliable, almost soft. The lieutenant was furious. In previous crushing fights, his success had depended on the victim struggling, making the body tense and thus more easily snapped.

In the fraction of a second that the man relaxed his grip and prepared for another sudden jerk that would have surely crushed both bowels and spine, Carter made his move.

With all his might, he clapped the palms of his hands over the man's ears, the third most vulnerable spot on the human body.

The lieutenant roared with pain. Carter spread his hands and gave the ears another mighty clap.

Even before Lieutenant Ospina roared from the second assault, Carter's fingers were at the man's eyes, digging deeply. As he felt the eyeballs beneath the clenched lids, he moved his right leg back and brought his knee crashing into the man's crotch.

With a screeching cry, Ospina literally flung Carter across the foyer and into the living room. Carter crashed into a heavy wooden coffee table and was momentarily stunned.

In the foyer, Lieutenant Ospina was still howling, holding his crotch with one hand and using the other in a vain effort to stop the pain in his eyes and ears.

Carter recovered quickly and came up for new action.

This time he wouldn't add to his own scar tissue by barreling into the big man. He picked up the heavy coffee table and, using it as a battering ram, ran across the room into the foyer, crashing the piece of furniture straight into the lieutenant's bent head.

The coffee table splintered. Ospina stood looking at his assailant with an intense hatred. His fingers worked in fury. He nodded once, as though deciding on what to do next to this upstart who had caused him so much pain, then began a long, slow fall toward the floor.

Nick Carter stood back and gave the man room. The big body slammed into the carpeted floor, jarring, it seemed, the whole wing of the building. Carter flicked Hugo into his palm and, reluctant to use it on such a formidable adversary when he was down, put the sharp point to the lieutenant's throat.

"I would not do that if I were you."

Carter didn't even have to look up to know that Colonel Emilio Sangre was holding a gun, and that the gun was pointed directly at his head.

He had heard of a Mexican standoff. But a Puerto Rican standoff?

FIFTEEN

"You should feel honored, Mr. Carter," the colonel said from behind the general's desk. "You will be the first man that I, personally, have killed."

Carter sat stolidly in the chair across the desk, his eyes on the colonel's eyes and on the Luger the man held in his hand. There had been no chance to disarm him. He had come out of a bedroom when Carter was smashing the lieutenant in the head with the coffee table and had won the Puerto Rican standoff handily.

Carter had had no choice but to drop the stiletto. When he had looked up and seen that Luger pointed at his head—and the hand holding it so steady and eager—he had given up. Not given up, he thought, merely marked time until a more favorable opportunity arose.

"I feel greatly honored," he said with acerbity. "And I'm certain that I won't be the last man that you, personally, will kill."

The colonel laughed. His eyes were filled with glee now. The big lieutenant was alive and would come around soon. As for his other officers and their failure to kill or contain the man from Washington, well, he would deal with that in time.

"This has been a good test," he said to Carter. "You have provided me with an excellent opportunity to weed

125

out the chaff, to separate my true followers from the mere hangers-on. The officers who stayed in their rooms while you wreaked havoc in the BOQ will face my wrath in time.''

"Not to mention your firing squad,'' Carter said.

"You read my mind well.''

"No. I've seen and smelled your type all over the world. Dictators are made of the same rotten cheese. The smell comes from a dying process that sets in the moment they decide to become dictators.''

The colonel's eyes narrowed with anger, but only briefly. He smiled at Carter.

"For a man who is about to die, you speak with a foul mouth. I really should have killed you the moment I saw you bending over Lieutenant Ospina, but I wish to know more about this strike force of yours in the mountains.''

"You mean your personal search team hasn't been able to find it? You're slipping, Tranquilo.''

The colonel's eyes narrowed, then sparkled with new glee. "So you know. And how did you find out?''

"Something Colonel Irena Balleta said,'' Carter told him.

"The bitch! How could she know?''

"She doesn't. But she told me that if the bomb were to be set off in San Juan, Los Bravos would be telling the American government that all Puerto Ricans were willing to die for independence. I couldn't buy that. I knew the moment I heard of this grisly plan that the military would take over Puerto Rico if any terrorist group from here set off an atomic bomb in San Juan. Or in any American city.''

"That is true,'' the colonel said. "But how did that lead you to suspect that I was Tranquilo?''

"Simple. If the military took over, the general would be in the catbird seat. From what I've observed, you pretty much run the general. In fact, he isn't in San Juan at all. He's still in Washington and you're in control. I don't know how you managed it, but it doesn't matter. The fact is, you're in control—for now.''

"And for always," the colonel said.

"That's doubtful, but we won't argue the point. Tell me, Colonel, how long do you figure it'll take you to parlay your edge into a full dictatorship? A year? Two? More?"

Carter was grinning at the colonel's obvious anger. Things weren't going as well now as he'd planned. But they would.

"You can be spared," Sangre said, leaning forward, his eyes taking on an anxious look. "You have proved that you are a fine warrior and a cunning, resourceful adversary. In the world that I will devise for Puerto Rico, you could be important."

"I'm listening."

The colonel smiled. "I knew you would. Look, my friend, this island has been a paradise since before it was seen by Columbus and plundered by Ponce de Leon. But only for a few. Rich as it is, it cannot give sustenance to the more than three million people who inhabit it. Riches are for the intelligent, the strong. All the others are cattle, there to help make the paradise even better for the ruling few. A man of your intelligence surely must know this worldly truth. It has been true since the fall of the ancient Greeks. It was true during the times of Great Pharoahs and Caesars. It was true—"

"During the Third Reich of Adolf Hitler?"

The colonel smiled again. A tight one. His anger was getting harder to contain. But he went on.

"People are cattle," he said, his voice gentle. "Surely you know that. They are children. Why did God make so many people without the basic intelligence to even make a living for themselves if men of intelligence did not show them how, set up systems and rules for them to follow? The strong, the intelligent, the resourceful, the courageous—these are the people who merit the riches that the world has to offer. Not the cattle. Have you not heard the phrase, 'Never cast pearls before swine'? It is a Biblical phrase. It has meaning for men like you and me. God meant for a few men to rule and for all other men to be ruled. Soft rulers lead the people down false trails, into poverty and confusion. Surely you can see that.''

Carter nodded. It was a truth taken out of context, a truth twisted to suit the ambitions of the man behind the desk.

''As the ruler of the new Puerto Rico, I can lead the people along the proper trails, remove the poverty and confusion, make them happy and well-off. In so doing, I shall make myself and my loyal lieutenants even more happy, more well-off. Peace and tranquility will reign on this paradise.''

''Now I know why the computer didn't pick up on your code name,'' Carter told the colonel. ''You hadn't planned to use it openly until you'd been made the military ruler and had set up your scheme to take over Puerto Rico. Only your closest associates used that name.''

''Correct. See what I mean about your value to me, Mr. Carter? Along with your courage and your personal strength, you have the ability to perceive. So few have that ability. A man of your talents could not fail to be my number one lieutenant.''

''It's a tempting offer,'' Carter said. ''Better than any I ever had.'' He let a smile appear on his lips as he caught the colonel's eyes and asked: ''What is it I must do to gain this powerful position in your new paradise?''

The colonel missed the note of disdain in Carter's voice. He was unable to perceive that the man from Washington was merely angling for time and opportunity. His pleasure at the man's seeming capitulation overcame all natural instincts.

''First, call off the strike force—or tell me where it is bivouacked. We must allow Alto Segundo to continue to function. I will report to Washington that you were killed by Los Bravos. I will hide you out at my villa on Cerro de Punta. When the time is right, you will be given another name—and untold riches.''

"You said the first thing was to call off the strike force and save the laboratory at Alto Segundo,'' Carter said, retaining the smile. "What's the second thing? And third, and so forth?''

The colonel pondered the questions. Delight still shone in his eyes, but he was no fool. Not a complete one, anyway. He decided to proceed cautiously with this man.

"We will get to many things in time,'' he said. "I would like you to tell me now, though, why you believed that man you killed at Alto Primero. You did not then suspect the truth about me. Why didn't you believe our intelligence reports that the bomb was to be taken to San Felipe and smuggled aboard a trawler? Especially when the trawler's existence was verified by ComSat?''

"I'm a gambler,'' Carter said lightly. "I played a hunch.''

The colonel nodded. He liked the answer, mostly because he preferred to believe that he'd done nothing tangible to make this man suspicious.

"Very good. Another plus in your favor. A man with infallible instincts. Tell me, Mr. Carter, did your hunch tell you of my plan to double-cross Jorge Menalos and the Communists by triggering the atomic bomb to go off at ten o'clock tomorrow morning instead of on Thursday?''

"It was in Jesus Damorcito's diary,'' Carter said calmly. He got the response he expected.

"Damn that traitor!'' the colonel stormed. "I knew he was keeping a journal—I should have killed him months ago! What else did he write in it? The location of the downtown building, no doubt.''

Carter grinned but said nothing. *Let the bastard think the worst,* he thought.

The colonel got up and began to pace. He kept the Luger in his hand, pointed in Carter's direction. He did a great deal of pondering as he paced. Finally he stopped and faced Carter from across the room.

"All right. It now becomes imperative that you join with me. If you want promises in writing, it will be done. If you refuse, I have no choice but to kill you. Now. I may not be able to save Alto Segundo from your strike force, but I will blow your pilot up when he arrives. I will have the time to get in touch with Jorge Menalos at—"

Two shots roared in the foyer. With peripheral vision, Carter saw the tongues of flame. His eyes shot toward the doorway, but he saw nothing. He looked back at the colonel in time to see the Luger drop to the floor, then the colonel's immense frame began to slump.

There was no glee in the colonel's eyes now. They were turning glassy. His mouth worked soundlessly, as though arguing with death. He fell headlong onto the floor. Dead.

Carter lost no time getting to that Luger. He had no idea who had shot the colonel. He didn't intend to be empty-handed when he found out.

He snatched up the Luger and came up in a firing stance as Colonel Irena Balleta walked into the room. She held a smoking .45 automatic in her right hand. The pistol was drooping toward the floor, as though the woman were about to faint.

"Irena! Why?"

"I heard—him—say that—he was—going—to kill—you." The words pulsed strangely from her lips. The .45 fell to the floor, followed immediately by her unconscious body.

Had she fainted, or was she wounded? Carter made a quick check of her body. There was only the superficial wound beneath her left breast, expertly bandaged by the base doctor. Irena's eyes fluttered, then opened wide.

"The colonel? Is he dead?"

"They don't come any deader. I appreciate your intentions, Irena, but your timing was rotten."

"What do you mean?" She sat up, saw the dead colonel, and shuddered.

"He was just about to tell me the location of the downtown building—where the atomic bomb is stashed."

"Good Lord! Oh, Nick, I'm sorry! I only heard—"

"Yeah, I know. Listen, we'd better get out of here. I have that miniature transmitter in my room, the one Josh Billings gave me. Let's get it, send the signal, and get the hell off this base. Once the colonel's death is discovered, we'll be getting flak from both sides of the fence—Sangre's loyal followers and the regular Air Force guys as well."

In the foyer, Carter looked around at the empty floor, puzzled. He stared at Irena.

"I left Lieutenant Ospina here, unconscious. You didn't see him when you came in?"

"I saw no one."

As they walked down the corridor, armed and wary, Irena told Carter how she'd heard the siren and gunfire, and had gone out to investigate. An officer had told her that it was some kind of exercise in combatting terrorism and told her to return to her quarters. Colonel's orders.

She'd returned, but the second round of gunshots made her suspicious that something was indeed wrong. She'd sneaked out of her room, gone to the quarters where Carter was billeted, and saw the devastation for herself.

"It was clearly no exercise," she said. "But I didn't suspect the colonel of being involved in your disappearance. I started looking for you, saw the general's door open, and went into the foyer. I heard Colonel Sangre talking about how he would take over Puerto Rico. I heard him offer you a job but knew from his tone that he was lying. When he said he would kill you now, I knew that I couldn't be loyal to a man like that. Even if you went along, even if he spared you to go along, I knew what I had to do. He wouldn't have lived up to his promises, you know."

"I know. I had no intentions of accepting his deal. But until you came along, I didn't know just what I'd do about the situation. I was still making plans, looking for an opportunity to move on him.''

"So I did right in killing him?''

"Yeah. It's just that your timing was bad.''

"I'm sorry, Nick. Truly sorry.''

They were at his room. The corridor was still full of bodies, still quiet. The three dead Los Bravos killers and the one phony MP were still in a pile in Carter's room. Carter fished out the transmitter, pressed the activator button, and started down the corridor with Irena.

At the juncture with the main corridor, Carter's sense of danger also became activated. It was all too quiet. And with Lieutenant Ospina on the loose, it shouldn't be this quiet.

The lieutenant had left the foyer, with Carter and the colonel talking not twenty feet away.

Where had he gone? And why?

Surely he would have alerted the colonel's other loyal officers, stirred them up, goaded them into some kind of action. If nothing else, the bodies of the Los Bravos men and the phony MPs and the two officers should have been whisked away, just in case some legitimate base officers stumbled across them and an investigation was started.

The silence in the BOQ corridors, and on the base at large, disturbed Carter. It was like a bomb that had stopped ticking and was in that millisecond of suspended time just before it went off.

When he and Irena stepped from the barracks and looked across the compound, there seemed to be no life at all out there. Just a rosy glow from the diversionary fire. But when they were halfway across the compound, Carter saw the running figures near the enlisted men's barracks.

"This way!'' he hissed, taking Irena's hand and reversing his course. "We can reach the fence behind the BOQ.''

The way was guarded by a mountain of a man in a uniform of Air Force blue. It was Lieutenant Ospina.

The huge man stepped from the shadows as Carter and

Irena rounded the corner of the BOQ. He held an automatic rifle in his hands, but he wasn't in position to fire it. He was in position to knock Carter and the colonel silly with the weapon.

"Christ," Carter muttered as the lieutenant drew back for a haymaker of a swing with the M-16. "Enough is enough."

He squeezed Wilhelmina's trigger. A tongue of flame flickered hotly in the night. A 9mm slug hurtled through the air and caught the big man in the face.

The M-16 kept coming, though. Carter and Irena ducked the blow. The lieutenant followed through with his swing. He smashed the weapon to pieces against the brick building, then tumbled on top of it, still as death.

The firing of the Luger seemed to be the signal for the other officers to act. They came in a swarm from the main doorway of the BOQ, fifty yards ahead.

Carter counted six of them in one group, plus two others straggling behind.

"You have five rounds left in that forty-five," he told Irena. "Use them now!"

Even before his final words had left his lips, he was crouched and firing. Wilhelmina worked beautifully, hurling out lethal charges that were accurate and deadly. Beside Carter, the big .45 barked and belched, throwing out fire and lead.

Carter's quick eye and faster mind counted four kills for him, two for Irena. The two stragglers, seeing the first group of men being riddled with bullets, stopped and made a hasty retreat. Carter let them go.

"This way!" he shouted to Irena.

She followed, running as fast as her lovely legs would take her. They crossed a narrow lawn, a roadway, ran between two administrative buildings, and headed for the chain link fence that was a hundred yards beyond the buildings.

Carter saw the tongues of flame before he heard the

reports of the rifles slinging out fire. He stopped and slammed his body on top of Irena, bowling her over.

A volley of lead whined above them, slamming into the side of a building. Carter worked quickly, pulling the woman around the corner to safety.

"I saw four weapons," he said. "M-sixteens, I'd guess. I'd also guess that the shots came from one of several squads. They've got us in a gauntlet situation. You feel like running any gauntlets?"

"I feel like going back to my room and going to bed," she replied, breathing hard. "Is your life like this all the time?"

"Only on the good days," he replied. He looked at the frightened woman crouched beneath him against the side of the brick building. "You know, this is very unfair to you. You could have stayed in your quarters and let me handle it. After all, you weren't involved with the colonel's plan. You and the other clean officers would be in the clear once this thing gets sorted out."

"Someone is trying to blow up my country," she said. "I'm as much a part of this as you are."

He studied her for a moment, admiring her. "Okay, then. It's run-the-gauntlet time."

Nick Carter took a running stance. He prepared his muscles for a hard, tough run to the fence.

He had a new clip in the Luger. The .45 Irena had picked up was empty. He'd have to plan and place his shots with incredible skill. He needed only to keep the men bearing the M-16 rifles a bit on edge, a bit scared, to destroy their aim.

Even then, all the odds were against him and Irena making and climbing that fence.

SIXTEEN

It would be a death run, Carter knew. There could be ten squads of the colonel's hand-picked soldiers out there along that fence.

But there was no chance at all inside. If the radio transmitter were working, sending its signal to Captain Billings up in the mountains, the pilot would home in on the signal and follow it. If he landed on the base, at the helipad, he'd be blown sky-high.

The colonel had been quite explicit on that point. Billings wouldn't know that he was flying into a trap. There was no way Carter could get that word to him.

He and Irena had to be outside the fence, far from the base, when the chopper arrived.

Even as Carter made his muscles go taut for the running start toward the fence, he heard the familiar chugging sounds of the Bell Cobra.

Dammit! Billings must have been waiting in the cockpit when the signal reached him. All he'd had to do was start the engine and take off.

"Too soon," Carter said under his breath. "Too damned soon!"

Maybe not. Maybe the demolition crew scheduled to blow up the helicopter was just now assembling. Maybe those men who came streaming out of the BOQ, only to be mowed down by Carter and Irena Balleta, made up the demolition crew. Either way, there was nothing to do but return to the compound.

"Cancel the gauntlet-run!" he barked to Irena. "We have to get back to the helipad. The pilot will be killed the second he sets that chopper down."

Irena ran behind him, keeping pace even though Carter was running full out. They crossed the road and the lawn, then circled the BOQ building.

The landing lights of the helipad went on suddenly, a welcoming gesture to the unsuspecting pilot above.

Carter watched the Cobra dip and turn, then swing its high tail around, working itself into a shuffling but smooth vertical descent. When the copter was only fifty feet above the pad, Carter ran forward, waving off Billings with one hand and firing at the ground-based landing lights with the other.

His aim was perfect. One light, then two lights, went out.

Captain Billings, alone in the copter, watched the strange scenario below. What the hell was Carter doing? Waving him off, or waving him down? And why was he firing a pistol? Billings saw the tongues of flame and heard the reports above the roar of the engine. Then he saw the two lights go out.

A third and fourth went out. The helipad was no longer a bright square of concrete with a circle and an X in its middle. A fifth light went out.

The squadron commander suddenly put it all together. A trap had been laid. He eased up on the collective pitch stick and let the Cobra hover there, thirty feet from the ground. He saw dark figures running around and heard more gunfire. A streaker of copper-sheathed steel punctured the metal behind his head. He swore aloud and flipped on his own landing lights. He ascended, tipped down the Cobra's nose, and eyeballed the scene below.

And saw Nick Carter in the center of the X, on his knees, firing at dark objects beyond the circle of the chopper's landing lights. Billings had unwittingly made the man a sweet target for unseen guns.

He cut the landing lights and began to lower the hook and cable. He eased into position directly over Carter's head, descended to thirty feet again, and listened to the hum of the winch motor.

Then Billings saw the woman come from out from the shadow of a building and saw her join Carter. He knew his prizes would be ripe targets as soon as they latched onto the hook. He couldn't let that happen.

And he couldn't land in that circle either. It was no doubt rigged for detonation—either on touchdown or by a hand generator located out of view.

So the captain moved ahead to a dark spot between two buildings and dropped the Cobra like a rock on the soft lawn. He left the motor at idle and ran to the rear. He opened the right side door just as Irena came dashing up.

"Welcome back," he chirped. "Where's the man from Washington?"

"I saw him run from the pad when you cut your lights," she gasped, panting as she climbed aboard with the pilot's help. "I'm certain he came this way."

"He damned well better have come this way," Billings said, picking up an M-16 he'd brought just in case. "There aren't any rescue aircraft anywhere else but right here."

Even as he spoke and lined the formidable weapon up on shadows he saw moving near the corner of a building, he saw a familiar shape slip into view. Carter was rounding an opposite building, setting a course for the Cobra.

Before Carter could move, however, the shadows from the other building darted into the open space, crouched, and took aim on the helicopter.

Billings wasted no time. He let fly with the M-16, raking the line of shadows with hot steel, giving Carter a chance to make a run for it.

Carter sprinted between the buildings. Billings watched him come, keeping his eye on the V of the M-16 barrel, watching for others. When Carter was ten feet from the open door, Billings put down the weapon and reached out to help.

The bellowing cry that rent the night startled and shocked all three of them: Carter, Billings, and Irena. It was a cry that was hardly human.

The creature that had uttered that inhuman cry sprang into the open, a pace behind the still running Carter. It was a big man in a lieutenant's uniform, his face a mask of blood.

Carter and the big, bloody man hit the door at the same time. Carter was kicking at the lieutenant, but the creature wouldn't be stopped. He was like something possessed.

"Shoot him!" Carter yelled above the clutching man's bellowing cries. "He's Lieutenant Ospina, one of the colonel's goons. Shoot the son of a bitch!"

The lieutenant was halfway in the door. He was kicking and bellowing and thrashing like one demented. Captain Billings picked up the M-16 but was reluctant to use it on a fellow Air Force officer—and he hadn't the slightest idea what the man from Washington was talking about. Who was the colonel?

The two were locked in a death grip. It was the wrong kind of death grip. The lieutenant had the grip, and Carter would soon have the death.

Irena sensed Carter's plight and understood why the pilot wouldn't fire. She snatched the rifle from him and brought it crashing down into the big man's face. The steel buttplate caught the lieutenant alongside the bullet hole that still oozed blood.

For an instant, nothing seemed to happen. Then the lieutenant rolled over and closed his eyes. And finally, his screaming mouth.

"Get us off the ground!" Carter ordered the pilot.

When Billings seemed reluctant, his eyes riveted to the bloody mess that was Lieutenant Ospina, Carter touched his shoulder. "Take my word for it, Josh. He's a goon, a traitor. Don't let the uniform fool you. Get us out of here or none of this will have meant a damned thing."

Carter shifted the lieutenant's body inside and left the door open as the helicopter rose in the night sky. A cluster of Colonel Sangre's men rounded a building and began to fire up at the Cobra.

It takes a lot to stir the bastards up, Carter thought as he took Pierre from his pocket and prepared it for a necessary task, *but once stirred, they don't know when to quit*.

He tossed the little gas bomb toward the rallying group and watched grimly as they began to die, swiftly, down there in the dark. By the time the Cobra was careening off toward the high mountains, Carter was already at work on Lieutenant Ospina, moving him into position alongside the open door.

"What are you going to do with him?" Irena asked.

"You'll see. He takes a lot of punishment but he's still alive. Where there's life, there's fear."

"I don't understand," she said.

"You will. It was you who gave me the idea of doing what I plan to do next."

He tied the big lieutenant's feet with strong nylon cord the pilot had in a supply case. He reached outside the gunship for the hook and cable, which he attached to the cord at the man's ankles. Then, with effort, he nudged the unconscious lieutenant out the door and onto the landing skid. He checked Irena's .45, found it empty, and gave her Wilhelmina.

"Keep your eyes on him. If he so much as moves a muscle, blow out whatever brains he has left."

"Nick, what are you going to do with him?"

"Remember you told me once that Sangre was an administrative officer because he was afraid of heights?"

"Yes, but what—"

"When I first came to Muniz, when we were down getting those aerial photos," Carter said, explaining patiently in spite of the whistling wind from the open door, "I checked the officer roster for Muniz. I saw Ospina's name. He's administrative. My guess is that he's just like his boss, the colonel. I intend to find out."

"But—"

Carter was already gone, up to the cockpit where he slid into the copilot's seat.

"Josh, you'll have to take this on faith," he said to the confused pilot. "The man back there is an animal. Colonel Sangre was an animal. There is a plan to incinerate thousands of people in downtown San Juan tomorrow morning, and the colonel and this man were a part of that plan. I need information and I need it quickly. Will you do what I ask?"

"To save thousands of people in San Juan? How could they be in danger?"

"I know this sounds incredible, but there is an atomic bomb stashed in a downtown building that is set to go off at ten o'clock tomorrow morning. I think this man may have vital information that could lead me to that downtown building."

"Holy shit," Josh Billings breathed, a determined expression slipping across his wide, homely face. "Just tell me what you want to do."

"Dangle the son of a bitch about fifty feet above the trees down there," Carter said. "If that doesn't make him talk, we'll think of something else."

"Brother," Captain Billings said. "I'd talk if you just *threatened* me with that kind of torture."

Five minutes later, Lieutenant Ospina stirred, moaned, and opened his eyes. And then he screamed.

He was lying on his back across a landing strut. His hands and feet were tied. Wind was howling through the struts and into his face. He looked up and saw Nick Carter's eyes above him.

He also saw—and felt—a big foot planted just beneath his chin. One tiny push and he knew that he'd go flying off that strut. The lieutenant had no idea how high they were flying. But any height at this speed would be fatal. He swallowed hard and stared back at the implacable eyes. He wouldn't grovel, wouldn't plead.

"If you've got nine lives, Lieutenant," the man above him snarled, "you've used up three or four of them already. I have one question. If you don't give the correct answer in one hell of a hurry, you'll use up the rest of your appointed nine lives in one hell of a bigger hurry. Now, where is the downtown San Juan building where the atomic bomb is being kept?"

Lieutenant Ospina managed to cough up phlegm into his mouth. He spat it at Carter. The wind whisked it away into darkness. Carter grinned. The lieutenant hadn't seen such a grin since he'd last looked into a mirror. A tiny arrow of fear pierced something inside, something sensitive.

"Wrong answer," Carter growled.

The foot kicked. Hard.

Lieutenant Ospina felt himself sliding along the skid, felt the wind take him. He was falling. *Madre de Dios*, he was falling into the jungle below!

He screamed. Not even his tough, enormous body could sustain a drop from an aircraft; for one split second, he wished he'd given the correct answer.

And then the slack went out of the cable, his rapid descent halted by a jarring jolt that rattled his teeth.

The howling wind. The streaking black jungle. The great bird of a chopper above. The pain. The fear.

That was the immediate world of Lieutenant Ospina.

"Let it all the way down to thirty feet," Carter called to Billings from the doorway. "Let him see the needles on the pine trees."

"I can make him eat some of them if you want," Billings shouted back from the pilot's seat.

"Just let him see them. Then bring him up for a repeat of the same question."

Captain Billings listened to the hum of the motor and watched the digital readout. He missed a beat and let the cable out to twenty-five feet. He missed the beat on purpose. *What the hell*, he thought. He'd give the screaming gorilla a really *good* look at the trees.

The scream from Lieutenant Ospina echoed up and down the dark valleys and hills. The Cobra, racing in a gentle slant up the hillside, kept a steady altitude.

Carter, Irena, and Billings could hear the scream, like one long sustained note from the world's loudest soprano, all the way inside the chopper.

"Jesus," Billings mused aloud, "you don't suppose I accidentally snagged his balls on a treetop?"

Carter grinned. "Sounds that way. Bring him up now."

The lieutenant felt the tug of the hook, then saw the trees drop away from sight. Never during his thirty years, not even when he'd endured the nightmares of childhood, could he recall ever being so frightened. A few more feet down and he'd have been shredded to raw meat in those trees.

If they were going to drop him, why didn't they drop him? he wondered through his terror.

When his huge body was lodged against the landing strut and he was staring up at the hard eyes again, he heard the question:

"Where is the downtown building where Menalos has the A-bomb?"

The lieutenant let fly a stream of colorful Spanish curses.

Carter grinned a cold, ghastly grin and said to the pilot:

"Let him back down."

"No!" the giant screamed back. "I will tell you! I will tell you what you ask!"

"All right," Carter shouted above the whistling wind. "Start telling."

"Bring me inside! Please! Bring me inside!"

And that is this man's weakness, Carter thought. *Other than his brain.*

Carter had a weakness too. Cruel and unusual punishment was not a part of his makeup. But it had come to a point where, as some politician had said, "Extremism in the defense of liberty is no vice."

Extreme measures were called for. The bomb would detonate automatically in less than twelve hours.

Carter and the special attack force had that much time to find the downtown site, then figure out a way to get in without triggering the bomb prematurely. It wasn't much time.

"Bring him in!" Carter yelled to the pilot.

Lieutenant Ospina was as good as his word. He gave the building's address—220 Avenida Caliente, just two blocks from Plaza de Colombo—and described the building: four stories, with administrative offices on the top floor, barracks for Los Bravos on the third, storage on the second, and export salesrooms on the first. He wasn't certain where the bomb would be, but he said there was a small laboratory in the basement, needed to set up the triggering device.

"But there's no need to hurry so much," Ospina said when he had stopped shivering from fright. "The bomb isn't set to go off until Thursday morning."

Carter looked into the man's eyes. And he realized Ospina was telling the truth as he knew it.

"So the colonel kept even you in ignorance," Carter told the man. "For your information, the bomb is set to go off at exactly ten o'clock this morning. They—"

He heard the gasp from Irena and turned to look at her. Her face was as white as chalk. Her eyes were wide, her mouth open.

"What is it, Irena? What's wrong?"

"I just remembered. That building. I have been there. Twice, I did favors for the colonel—delivered papers for him to San Juan Exports at two-twenty Avenida Caliente."

"You were inside?"

"Yes. To the top floor, to the administrative offices."

"You've seen Menalos?"

"I'm not sure if he was the man I talked to. But I do know one thing: this man is telling the truth. He described the building perfectly."

"Right," Carter said, his sense of danger warning him that something was amiss here. He left Irena with the lieutenant and went into the cockpit. Billings looked at him, puzzled by the look on the agent's face.

"Problems?"

"Maybe. Let's get this crate to the bivouac area and organize a strike on Alto Segundo. I have to give that downtown building more thought. Among other things."

"Can I help?"

"No," Carter said, "unless you can read minds."

SEVENTEEN

Even as Nick Carter studied the maps and photographs laid out on the portable planning table in the big tent, his mind was on Irena. There were unresolved questions.

With the attack force, Carter had been studying the defenses of Alto Segundo—known to Puerto Ricans as the lonely old monastery called Alto Beneficio—for the better part of an hour. A part of that time had been devoted to a discussion of the downtown building where the atomic bomb lay ticking away the precious minutes.

It was now 1:30 A.M. In just eight and a half hours, unless Nick Carter or a member of the attack force—or perhaps Irena—had a plan to stop it, the bomb would go off.

The man named Santiago had been sure of one thing: the building was safe from interference. Carter remembered the dying young guard's words: "It is said that Menalos will have the bomb rigged in such a way that the slightest interference, even the breaking in of a door at his premises, will cause it to blow up immediately. Even if you drop a conventional bomb on top of the building, it will go off."

The decision, agreed on by Captain Josh Billings and his other pilots and crews, had been made to assault Alto

Segundo and destroy its bomb-making capabilities, then to take on the downtown building. In preparation for both, a fast helicopter had been dispatched stateside to pick up a sensitive hand-held Geiger counter.

Carter would have to be absolutely certain that the laboratory held no raw plutonium before he set charges to blow up the place as he'd done at Alto Primero. At that time, he hadn't used a Geiger counter; all the experts on the subject had insisted that the plutonium would be inside the bomb, not on the premises. They had been right, but they hadn't counted on the spare plutonium that was now on the trucks headed for San Felipe. And there could be even more, stashed at Alto Segundo.

Beyond that, Carter would need the Geiger counter to help him find the atomic bomb if and when he got inside the downtown premises of San Juan Exports.

"Okay, guys," Carter said, leaning back and pressing his fingertips to his aching temples. "It's settled. As soon as the courier chopper returns with the Geiger counter, we hit Alto Segundo. I'll take the ground approach; you keep to the air."

There was nodding, but not any enthusiastic approval. Captain Billings and two of his pilots had insisted that all of them keep to the air and use devices aboard the helicopters to check for radiation. Carter had insisted that any plutonium at the laboratory would be kept deep underground in a lead-lined vault. The devices aboard the aircraft, no matter how sensitive, wouldn't pick up the trace.

The only way to take Alto Segundo was the way he'd taken the first lab—by going in on foot. Carter had refused Josh Billings's offer to accompany him up the western wall; Carter had opted to go alone. He explained that the wall was too high for rope and hook. He'd have to scale it, and he had only one set of climbing tools.

"We can radio the pilot going for the Geiger counter," Billings had suggested. "He could pick up another set."

"Negative, Captain. I do this alone."

Carter wasn't playing the hero, although he knew the chances were good that an inexperienced fighter like Josh Billings might never make it through an assault on the mountaintop lab. He was actually being selfish. Carter knew the young captain would make mistakes, mistakes that could give them both away and cause one Nick Carter to buy the farm. He'd avoided ever present death on too many assignments to let an inexperienced man blow it for him now.

Carter began folding the maps and slipping the photos into manila envelopes.

"We have an hour or two before we head out," he said, looking around at the weary pilots and crewmen. "I suggest we make good use of it and get in some sack time."

There was enthusiastic approval of that suggestion. The men filed out of the command tent. Billings stayed until the last.

"Sure you won't change your mind, sir—I mean Nick? Those people have been warned by now. They'll be waiting for you."

"They'll be waiting for a man," Carter said with a grin, "not a mountain goat. Only a mountain goat would try to climb that wall, right?"

"Yeah," the homely pilot agreed. "And he wouldn't make it."

"This one will. Get some sleep, Josh."

"Yes, sir."

Nick Carter lay back on his cot and stared at the soft glimmer of firelight through the tent flap. The fire they'd used to prepare a late meal was dying now, but enough remained to fling eerie shadows across the ceiling of the tent. Carter thought idly of Lieutenant Ospina, now on his way to Miami for medical attention and intensive interrogation. *The big bastard will live to go to prison. He probably has nine more lives left in that massive body.*

And then his thoughts drifted slowly back to Irena Balleta, who was presumably sleeping in the adjacent tent. His mind wanted to go over the questions he had about her, but he had tried to keep his mind off that subject. He was successful only for a time.

Had she set him up at El Palacio? Was her half brother, whom she claimed to detest, supposed to have killed the man from Washington so that the conspirators could go on with their plans unhindered? And wasn't it uncanny how Antonio Vortez and his thugs just happened to get into that big limousine and follow them up into the hills, choosing just the right road? What about what happened at the Escobar farm? Was Nick Carter supposed to have died along with Maria, the woman who supposedly reared Irena when she became an orphan?

Other questions involved the loss of the special radio and the way Irena just happened to show up at the crucial moment to kill Colonel Sangre—just when the man was about to reveal the location of the downtown building. And what about Irena's gasp in the helicopter when Lieutenant Ospina was told that the bomb was to go off at ten in the morning and not on Thursday? Perhaps these questions weren't so minor.

Then again, he thought with a weariness that floated through his bones and made his joints ache, perhaps he was jumping at shadows. In the three critical situations—at El Palacio, on the road up the mountain, and at Maria Escobar's farm—Colonel Irena Balleta was just as much a target for death as Nick Carter had been.

In Carter's long career as a Killmaster for AXE, he had met many women and had loved a good number of them. He seemed drawn to interesting women, and they to him. Some of those women had betrayed him, though most had done it with a great deal of regret. Regret or not, a betrayal was a betrayal. He could have lost his life each time.

Carter knew that his weakness for women carried one

enormous flaw: he was unable to determine until it was almost too late whether they were being truthful or were planning to betray him. *Well, hell,* he thought, *how can any man determine such a thing?* All he knew, as he lay on the cot and felt his exhausted body ache for rest and sleep, was that he wanted to see Irena just one more time before he set off on tonight's mission to Alto Segundo.

He got up and went to her tent. The flap was open, and she lay under a blanket on her narrow cot. Mosquito netting was not needed at this altitude, but blankets were. Her long golden hair fell across the top of the cot and hung almost to the floor of the tent. She was asleep, he was certain, and she looked positively angelic in the innocence of sleep.

"Irena?" He shook her shoulder gently, aroused by the feel of her soft flesh under the fatigue jacket. "Wake up. I need to talk to you."

"Nick? What is it? Are you getting ready to leave?"

Irena had begged to go along on the mission, but Carter had flatly denied her request. He had also excluded her from the planning session with Billings and the others of the attack force. Had it been a lack of trust, or had he been trying to spare her from danger? He didn't know. There was so much he didn't know about this lovely woman, or his feelings for her.

"No. I need to talk to you."

She sat up, gathering the blanket around her, clasping her legs with her arms. Carter sat at the end of the cot, his hands folded across his thighs. His usual ease with women was gone; he didn't know just how to approach the subject with Irena.

"Yes," she said after studying his troubled face. "Yes, I believe you do need to talk to me. The question is, will you believe what I say to you?"

"What's that supposed to mean?" He looked at her levelly, his eyes trying to be hard but softening as they met her eyes in the gentle firelight from outside.

"You don't trust me, Nick," Irena said. "That's painfully clear and has been at various points all along the way. I once told you that I wouldn't trust Colonel Sangre if I were you. I said I wouldn't even trust me. In some ways you've followed that advice, but you want to trust me. And there were times, my dear Nick, when your life literally was in my hands, as mine was in yours."

"That's true." For one thing, he thought, she could have killed him when she shot Colonel Sangre. She could have shot him with Wilhelmina up there in the chopper when he was forcing Lieutenant Ospina to talk. There must have been other times, but he couldn't think of them now. The fact was, she had passed up chances to kill him and she hadn't done it. So why did he doubt her, why was there *any* lack of trust?

"All I can say," Irena told him, "is to trust your instincts. If you have doubts about me, go with them. I can tell you that I'm not one of the colonel's lackeys. I had no knowledge of his plans. If I had, I would have reported them to people who would have eliminated the threat the colonel has posed. I don't ask you to believe me. I only ask you to trust your own instincts."

"Right now," Carter said with a grin, "my instincts tell me that I'm a prize horse's ass. I've already decided that you're vital to the second phase of tonight's operations, so why do I keep vacillating about whether or not to trust you?"

She sat upright, staring at him in the faint light. "What have you decided that concerns me, Nick? How can I help in the second phase, whatever that is?"

"I'd rather tell you later," he said, reaching out to touch a lock of her long hair. "Right now, I have something else in mind."

"Yes?"

He moved closer, feeling the heat of her body, noticing that she moved toward him at the same time. He put his hand on her cheek, then leaned and kissed her full lips.

Her hands slipped around his waist, being careful not to touch the place where his own wound was just starting to heal.

"You should have come with me to the sick bay at Muniz," she said, nodding toward his side wound. "You need proper medication and a better bandage on that."

He gingerly touched the bandage high on her side, near the swell of her breast. "We sound like a couple of geriatrics," he said, "talking about our infirmities. I'm more interested in our vitality, our energy. . . ."

"And our passion?"

"That too."

"Oh, Nick, I'd hoped you would come to me before you left on this suicide mission. I didn't think you would—I know how you need the sleep and the rest—but I really hoped and prayed that you would."

"I guess I knew all along that I would come."

"Even though you haven't resolved how you really feel about me, about whether or not you can trust me completely?"

"That's something else we can put off until later," Carter said, his hands moving up to cup her perfect breasts, his fingers gently massaging her hardening nipples. "Let's get back to that passion you mentioned."

She came into his arms, and he kissed her deeply. Their tongues probed each other's mouths. Irena lay back on the narrow cot and Carter moved alongside her, one leg draped over her thighs, his chest pressing against her breasts.

The cot was nowhere near as plush and comfortable as the big bed in her apartment, but neither seemed to care. Passion rose, and with its rise, Carter felt his fatigue slipping away. Years slipped away. He was the young stallion, the eternal stud, the tireless and relentless lover.

"My God but you are good with a woman," Irena cried as he entered her. "So strong, yet so gentle. So passionate, yet so tender. Let the strength and the passion rule,

Nick. Make me know that on this night of fear and appre-
hension that I have been truly made love to.''

He did as he was told.

Later, spent, satiated, they lay in each other's arms and
slept. They were still there when a slightly embarrassed
Captain Josh Billings came in and woke them up to tell
Carter that it was time to go. Time to carry out the assault
on Alto Segundo.

As Carter left the tent, he caught Irena's eyes. They
were large and moist, as though she might cry at any
second. He tried to read what was behind those eyes and
was convinced that if he didn't leave soon, she really
would burst into tears. She was afraid for him, and that
was a very good sign.

The guard was sleepy, but he dared not sleep. Sleeping
on duty meant instant death. But there was no way that
madman from Washington could reach Alto Segundo the
way he'd reached, penetrated, and destroyed Alto Primero.

The walls on three sides of the old monastery were two
hundred feet high. The fourth side had an electrified
fence, guard dogs, a wide strip of closely spaced mines,
and sharpshooting Los Bravos with those excellent
Kalashnikov rifles. The colonel had gathered all the
sharpshooters in the country at Alto Segundo within hours
after Alto Primero had been blown up.

The guard sat on the top of the wall and gazed at the
dark jungle below. Far away was a glow in the sky. It was
the lights of San Juan reflecting off low clouds. The guard
felt warmed by the glow and wished he were there, in a
cantina, drinking and fondling some soft, willing woman.
He yawned, knowing that all his dreams were unreacha-
ble. For now.

Once independence came, he'd been told, there would
be plenty of free time, plenty of beer, and plenty of eager
women for all who had proved their loyalty to the cause.

He and the others had been promised that by a number of leaders. Colonel Emilio Sangre. Jorge Menalos. Antonio Vortez. Jesus Damorcito. The guard didn't know which of the four would become the top leader once independence came. He didn't care. No matter who became top man, the promises had been made. They would be kept.

And yet, even on this remote, lonely mountaintop where there were no women, no beer, no joy, and no revelry, he'd heard rumors of a struggle among the leaders. He'd heard, mostly from Rosario the rumormonger, that Antonio Vortez and Jesus Damorcito were dead. Victims of the man from Washington. Rosario had also said that the gringo had killed three guards at Alto Primero. Sometimes Rosario was right, and his rumors proved to be true.

But the guard didn't believe the story that the madman had scaled the seventy-foot wall of Alto Primero. Even if such a story were true, there was a vast difference between seventy feet and two hundred feet. Nobody, man or beast, could scale this wall, even if he climbed the tallest tree below and started from there.

The guard peered down the side of the smooth wall, looking for signs of a resourceful superman who might prove him wrong. He saw a shadow fifty feet below and to the right. The shadow seemed to be moving. He looked up, saw the moon cross an open space of clouds, and grinned when he realized that the movement below had been the shadow of a cloud. He looked below. With the moon behind another cloud, the guard saw nothing. No shadows. Not even the thin lines delineating the huge stones that made up the wall.

The guard turned on the wall and faced the dark yard leading to the central buildings. Small trees alternately cast long shadows and disappeared as the moon passed behind clouds. Yes, the moving shadow on the wall had been a reflection from the moon, an image created by the moon's light, the way a candle reflects the shape of a woman's body against a tent wall.

Marvelous shapes, indeed, had the women of Puerto Rico. The guard didn't like the skinny ones who copied the shapes and styles from the mainland. He liked his women plump to the point of fatness. He liked enormous hips, wide expanses of rich brown skin, and great breasts with large dark aureoles and nipples.

He couldn't get his thoughts off women. He thought of making love, of how satisfied and sleepy he was after making love—especially after he'd drunk a lot of wine or beer. He lay back on the wall and watched the moon dart between the cumulocirrus clouds that filled the sky.

He couldn't sleep. He mustn't sleep. But there was no chance that anyone could scale this high wall. It was impossible. No man ever had and no man ever would. If he had been chosen to be among the sharpshooters guarding the fence and main gate, there would be no question that he must stay awake, be alert.

But here, on top of the east wall that dropped a sheer two hundred feet to the steep, hilly jungle, there was less reason to waste such a perfect night by indulging in silly daydreams. Real dreams, those that came from sleep, were best.

In his real dreams, he often found himself in bed with hugely plump women with wide hips and enormous brown breasts. And that, he knew, was normal for a young man of nineteen, even if he was a full-fledged member of Los Bravos.

The guard closed his eyes for a moment. A real dream began. He was behind a bench in Plaza de Colombo, lying naked in the cool grass. Clutched warmly to his naked body was Narisa. She was as plump as he liked, with breasts like cannonballs, and he was sucking on one of her brownish-red nipples.

The guard could hear only the roaring of his passion. He could not hear the soft *tunk, tunk, tunk* that came from just below him. He could not hear the soft, muted scrapings or the gentle jingling of snaps and buckles.

The guard was trying to work Narisa's entire cannon-ball breast into his mouth when he heard a soft, gentle jangling and decided that it was the jangling of Narisa's many bracelets.

And then he felt something tighten on his throat, felt his head being pressed against the ground. It hurt, but soft grass shouldn't hurt like that. It was the wall. He clung to the dream, hoping the pain in his throat would go away.

"One sound and I break your neck."

Who was talking? It was a man's voice. It was tough and mean, like the *policia* sometimes. Had a policeman found him and Narisa behind the bench?

The thing around his neck tightened, and the dream faded altogether. He opened his eyes and saw a pair of cold, hard eyes staring into his. He saw and felt the hands against his jaws, and knew that the man with the hard eyes was holding a garotte around his neck. With one impulsive jerk, the garotte could crush his trachea, even break his neck.

Who was this man? Where did he come from?

The man wore all black. He even wore a hood over his dark hair. His face was smudged with black stuff. But the eyes reflected moonlight, appearing like the eyes of a Satan-possessed fiend.

The guard saw bandoliers of ammunition crisscrossing the man's chest, saw grenades hanging from a belt, saw the enormous rifle barrel with a huge sight jutting above the man's shoulders. He saw white rope coiled around one big shoulder.

The guard felt like screaming despite the warming. It must have shone in his eyes. The garotte went tighter, and he could not scream. He could barely breathe.

"You have ten seconds to tell me which part of the monastery houses the laboratory for the building of the bombs," the man's gravelly voice commanded.

"I—can-cannot—breathe," the guard gasped.

The garotte eased on his throat. He took in a deep breath and was prepared to scream when the man apparently read his mind again and tightened the thin loop of steel wire. The scream died.

"Once more. Tell me where the laboratory is located. Is it underground?"

The garotte relaxed, and the guard decided not to test this man's satanic powers any longer. Or his strength.

"They build the bombs in the former wine cellar. In the south wing, two floors below the earth."

The man held the garotte in place and swiveled his head to survey the low dark buildings. He studied the south wing for a long time.

"Is that the door to the wine cellar?" the man asked. "The white one that looks like a church door?"

"That is the door. Who are you? How did you get here?"

The man grinned. There was no promise in the grin. No humor. No indication that the man was any happier with the information he'd been given.

"Just do as you're told," Carter said, "and answer my questions quickly and truthfully unless you want to be thrown off this wall."

The questions came one after another. How many guards were at Alto Segundo? Where were they placed inside and outside the monastery buildings? Was the laboratory heavily guarded? Who lived in the other wings? Were munitions kept in the monastery? The guard rattled back answers.

There were a hundred and fifty guards. Fifty were guarding the southern fence, four were guarding the walls, and the others were asleep. There were no guards in or around the laboratory. The other guards and their sergeants lived in the other wings, along with a few technicians who were doing the menial tasks involved in the building of the bombs. There was a room beneath the sergeants' barracks that housed extra land mines, many grenades, some bazookas, and a great heap of TNT.

"Where is the plutonium kept?"

"In a lead-lined room beside the old wine cellar. It was once a storm cellar, a shelter from the terrible hurricanes that sweep the Caribbean in later summer and early fall. How did you get up here? The fence is heavily guarded and there is a minefield just outside it. It is impossible to scale the wall!"

The man with the hard eyes and gravelly voice smiled. Was there promise or hope in the smile? The guard couldn't tell. The man held the garotte with one hand and produced a wooden mallet with the other. He showed the mallet to the guard, then showed him pitons. Mountain-climbing tools. But that was impossible. That was. . . .

The guard recalled the little *tunk, tunk, tunk* sounds, the jangling, the scraping. He recalled the moving shadow he had thought was the shadow of a cloud being moved by the moon. That shadow had been this man.

And he knew who the man was. This was the man from Washington, the man the leaders had feared, the man who had killed three guards at Alto Primero and had destroyed the laboratory there. The man who, perhaps, had killed Antonio Vortez and Jesus Damorcito.

Rosario's rumors were true.

The man was here to do more killing. He would succeed because the guard had slept and dreamt of Narisa.

"What will you do with me?" he asked, feeling courage rise as he remembered that he was part of Los Bravos, pledged to die for the cause.

Carter felt a sick feeling at the pit of his stomach. There was a moral decision to be made here. In the thick of battle, he would have blown away this young man without much more than a second thought. Only a kid would have taken his duty so lightly and gone to sleep on top of the wall. Fortunately for Carter, the guard had done what no seasoned professional soldier would have done. Carter had counted on that. Most of the lower echelon of Los Bravos were made up of simple, brainwashed kids.

Carter tied the guard with the nylon rope, stuffed his mouth with his handkerchief, and tied his scarf around his face to keep him silent. He lay the guard just inside the raised wall, in total darkness.

Carter pressed the button on the small radio transmitter and heard the squadron commander's voice: "Carter, where are you?"

"Just got inside. Lucky break with a sleeping guard. The lab is in the south wing, but there's a hitch. A veritable munitions dump is located in the central sector, too close to the room where the radioactive materials may be kept. As soon as I check things out, I'll signal back. Make your first run over the south wing to destroy the lab, and your secondary strike on the other wings."

He stopped, gazed around the yard, and spotted a guard walking at the northern end of the mountaintop yard. The guard was two hundred yards from the nearest wing. Near the guard was a small stone building, perhaps a guard shanty.

It would be his sanctuary during the strike. He moved toward the northern sector, toward the guard. He'd gone only fifty feet when he heard the low snarl behind him. He turned and was looking directly into the little red eyes of a monstrous Doberman.

The vicious guard dog was already crouched to spring.

EIGHTEEN

The dog sprang before Nick Carter had Hugo firmly in hand. As the sharp canines clamped over his right wrist, his fingers reflexively relaxed and the stiletto went flying into the dark grass.

Carter looked around wildly for the guard that must be accompanying the dog, then realized that the dogs were apparently allowed to run loose, trained to attack anyone who didn't smell familiar.

The absence of an armed guard was no solace. The dog, unsatisfied with Carter's wrist, let go, backed off, let out a grinding snarl, and went for his throat.

It was then that Carter's reflexes outmatched the dog's. He made a flying leap onto the grass, found Hugo's handle, and came up with the razor-sharp blade. He buried it in the dog's chest, pulled it out, and neatly cut the animal's throat.

Working swiftly, knowing that other dogs would pick up the scent of freshly spilled blood, he carried the dog to the wall and tossed the body over. He knelt, scanned the entire yard with the sniperscope, saw no more dogs—or guards—and headed north again, toward the stone shanty and the guard he'd seen earlier.

Ignoring the pain in his bleeding wrist, Carter eased up behind the patrolling sentry. When the guard turned to make the eastern leg of his rounds, Carter was on him, arcing Hugo's lethal blade around his soft neck, opening a spillway of blood. Carter hefted the guard's body over the wall to join the big Doberman in the jungle below.

Carter checked the guard shanty. It was empty of humanity. There was a small radio on a table, a wooden chair, a stack of dirty books, a sawed-off 20mm cannon shell for an ashtray, a low cot, a pair of binoculars, and a rack of automatic rifles. Carter counted twenty rifles. He removed the rounds from each of the curved clips and jammed the clips back into the AK-47 rifles. He went to the north wall and threw the cartridges into the darkness below.

During a coldly methodical stroll, Carter swiftly dispatched the other two guards assigned to duty on the three walls. He avoided the fence area, unwilling to attract the attention of more dogs. His right arm was already throbbing all the way to his shoulder, but blood had stopped oozing from the two punctures.

When the last of the guards had been killed, Carter turned his attention to the cathedral-style door in the south wing. He went to it, blew off the lock after wrapping Wilhelmina in canvas to muffle the noise, and went inside.

Once his eyes had adjusted to the deeper darkness, he checked out offices on the main floor. There were draftsmen's tables and a whole library of scientific books. Carter snapped on a tiny red-glowing flashlight and checked the titles. All the books pertained to nuclear weapons.

The bulk of the literature was U.S. government pamphlets put out by the Atomic Energy Commission. There were also textbooks with long, cryptic titles. And there were popular books: *Atoms at Your Service*, *Perils of the Peaceful Atom*, *The Careless Atom*, *The Silent Bomb*, *Day of Trinity*, *Atompower*, *Assault in Norway*, *No High Ground*.

Even the books written by authors who proposed the atom for peaceful uses, especially in nuclear power plants, provided pertinent information on how to use the atom for nonpeaceful purposes. Carter shook his head at the vast array of dangerous reading and went below.

On the next level down were more offices and two small laboratories. Carter recognized some of the equipment: an electromagnetic diffuser used to enrich and separate certain waste materials into usable, weapons-grade plutonium 239; and a gaseous diffusion oven for smelting beryllium and polonium, two necessary elements in the detonation of an implosion-type atom bomb.

There were molds used to make the gold and platinum shields to house the core of subcritical plutonium. Carter found traces of the precious metals in the thick, heavy molds. There were test tubes, beakers, and bunsen burners. With some notable exceptions, he knew, the labs could pass for college chemistry classrooms.

Carter thought of men like Enrico Fermi and Werner von Braun and Albert Einstein, and found himself wondering if those men, who had worked in labs much like these, had had even a glimmer of an idea of what their discoveries would do to the twisted minds of men of lesser intelligence and greater ambition.

If they had known, would they still have probed the mysteries of the atom and given birth to the one single weapon that man could use to destroy himself and the planet on which he lived?

They had known, he concluded. But in the name of science, they had proceeded. Science understood, but would God?

Nick Carter would bet that they would stand in no better stead on Judgment Day than men like Colonel Sangre or Jorge Menalos. Or, for that matter, Adolf Hitler, whose mad rush to create the first atomic bomb had set Carter's own country on a go-for-broke effort to create it first.

For that matter, how would he, Nick Carter, stack up?

He had certainly killed many men in his life.

Carter gave up such questions and descended to the third level. Here, the equipment was far more sophisticated, and larger. And more cryptic. Carter recognized four large metal containers as the outer shells of crude atomic bombs. He'd seen photos of actual bombs. The shells were frighteningly similar.

The metal shells, each about the size of a small desk, were far from empty. The bomb-building business had been booming.

Carter saw the yoke that would hold the gold- and platinum-clad core of subcritical Pu-239. Placed in a set pattern around the center of the yoke were the packets of TNT. Timing devices had been installed but not yet attached to the TNT. Red, white, and green wires stuck out like the legs and arms of a struggling octopus.

Recalling previous briefings on the detonation of an atomic device, Carter could imagine what would happen at the fateful moment. The packets of TNT would be detonated, and the explosion, perfectly timed and ringing the core of subcritical Pu-239, would compress the fissionable material into a critical mass.

To enhance the resulting explosion and chain reaction, neutrons from the radioactive beryllium and polonium would be released from the "urchin," a tiny pouch in the center of the Pu-239 core, to bombard the plutonium nuclei.

The result? A blast of indescribable, almost incalculable proportions.

The plutonium bomb dropped on Nagasaki had only a ten percent efficiency rating, yet the explosion was equal to that of twenty thousand tons of TNT.

The bombs Carter saw under production in this mountaintop laboratory were identical in size to the Nagasaki bomb, but he could see that the efficiency rating would be considerably higher, perhaps as much as fifty percent.

A hundred thousand tons of TNT!

And, Carter thought, it was all so simple.

The most awesome weapon the universe had ever seen boiled down, quite simply, into a mechanical device that without conscience or complexity could open the secrets of the universe—and ultimately destroy it.

The most frightening and dangerous Pandora's box ever conceived in the mind of man.

He found the lead-lined room easily. Above the steel door was an enormous sign: *PELIGRO—MATERIALES RADIOACTIVOS*.

Carter didn't need his knowledge of Spanish to know that the sign was a warning against the presence of radioactive materials. The Pu-239 was or had been in that room. Carter backed away and unsnapped the small Geiger counter from a webbed belt. He activated it and moved closer to the steel door. The device began to click, slowly, and a needle rose slightly from the negative range. Even when he had the Geiger counter up against the door itself, the clicking and needle movement were minimal.

The next step, he knew, was to open that door. He had no protective clothing and knew that a certain amount of radioactivity would remain even if the plutonium had been removed. It probably wouldn't be sufficient to cause any damage to his body. But if the plutonium were indeed inside and he opened that door without protection, he could expect a slow frying that would destroy him in a matter of days.

Carter made a quick search of the laboratory and found several small suits that looked as though they had been used as protective garb. They revealed a certain amount of radiation. He tried one, found it too small, and went to others. They were all too small.

It didn't matter, he decided. The plutonium was aboard one of those trucks en route to San Felipe. He was certain of it. But certain enough to stake his life on it?

He could still have Captain Billings pick him up and then strike the lab with rockets and bombs. Once that munitions cache was hit, the whole place would be scattered for miles across the jungle below. And if the plutonium were behind that steel door, it also would be scattered over that jungle.

Nick Carter, fighting back a lump in his throat and an incessant pounding in his chest, grasped the handle of the steel door and turned it. He held the Geiger counter ready. If the clicking increased steadily, he would slam the door and hope that exposure had been minimal and unharmful.

Jesus, he muttered, *how do I get into such situations? Why don't I retire, buy a real farm somewhere in Colorado, and settle down to a life of whittling toys for my grandchildren, even though I don't have any grandchildren?*

Aware that Josh Billings and his men were somewhere up in the sky a discreet distance away waiting for his signal, Carter suddenly turned the door handle and pulled the steel door open a few inches. He shot the Geiger counter forward into the crack. The clicking increased, but only slightly. The needle rose, but it remained in the safe range.

He'd been right. The plutonium was gone; it was aboard one or both of those trucks. As soon as he had the chance, he'd get word to Hawk to have the trucks picked up, just as he'd suggested that a military group be sent to Muniz to mop up the remaining officers who'd been part of Emilio Sangre's gang.

Carter breathed a sigh of relief and wiped the sweat from his forehead, then closed the door. He left the laboratory and went quietly through dark corridors, his smudged face and black suit blending nicely with the old monastery's underground murkiness.

The munitions were exactly where the young guard had said they would be, but Carter was amazed at the quantity—especially of TNT. Sangre must have planned to make plenty of small nuclear bombs, and his Puerto Rico would become, in effect, another member nation in the nuclear club. Well, Carter mused, that was all over now.

Outside, Carter looked for the safest haven when the holocaust came to this mountaintop. When Billings and team struck, and those munitions went off, there might not be *any* safe place. The sleeping guard contingent, he figured, would make a break for the northern end, if only to avoid the minefield. If a stray bomb set off a few of those mines, they could all blow, making the rest of the compound highly dangerous.

As for Carter, he'd already picked out his haven. He ran in a crouch to the wall where he'd left the young guard tied and gagged. He attached a length of nylon rope under the guard's arms, lowered the man over the side of the wall, and tied the free end of the rope to the trunk of a nearby tree.

Working slowly and methodically, he cut another length of rope for himself. He tied one end to the same tree and the other around his chest. Once he'd lowered himself over the side, he drove in four pitons and latched his lifeline snaplock onto them.

If the fire and destruction destroyed the nylon ropes, the pitons would at least keep him safe. There was nothing more he could do for the young guard.

Then again, the explosions could blow out this whole section of wall, bringing certain death to them both.

Carter nestled the Weatherby on top of the wall, stood on two pitons, and swept the area with the sniperscope. Red images filled his brain. The fence with roving dogs and patrolling guards. The dark villa. The guard shanty at the northern end. The trees and bushes.

He would see the guards and technicians come running out of the villa when the helicopters struck. He had a clear field of vision. Carter knew he would not be a mere bystander in the inferno to come.

He put down the Weatherby and radioed the squadron commander. He lowered himself beneath the top of the wall to make certain his voice didn't carry across the yard.

After explaining the entire layout, Carter gave Billings
the strike tangents.

Bombs and rockets were to strike the 27th parallel they
had worked out on the grids of the photos of this mountaintop. Machine gun fire was to be directed at the 24th
parallel, then at the 36th parallel.

These tangents represented the area of the chain link
fence, the south wing with the laboratories, and the northern end of the mountaintop.

Carter checked his watch. It was precisely 2:51.

"Give me an ETA."

"Yes, sir," the pilot's voice crackled back. "It's now
2:51. ETA will be 3:02. First strike, on twenty-seventh
parallel, will be 3:02:09."

"Go!"

Carter returned the radio to a pocket and took up the
Weatherby again. He turned to look at the guard. The
young man was hanging like a rag doll less than three feet
away. His large black eyes were regarding the Killmaster
as he probably would his God. With reverence and fear.

The guard knew that this man had come to destroy the
laboratories and all the men inside the villa. But why was
he going to so many pains to preserve the life of one
insignificant guard? He did not understand the man in the
black suit.

"Hang in there," Carter said softly, almost chuckling
at his own grim humor. "With luck, we'll both make it
through this."

At precisely 2:59:06, Carter's ears caught the soft
throbbing of helicopter rotors on the moist morning air.
He alternately watched the sky and his watch.

Carter saw the three Cobras come. They angled in from
the north, cut wide to the west, and came in directly over
the minefield and the chain link fence. Their running
lights twinkled like multicolored fireflies in the black sky.

Carter counted off the seconds and milliseconds. At
3.02:09, he saw two great tongues of flame leap from the

flagship copter. As much as he wanted to see the pyrotechnics, he ducked his head beneath the level of the wall.

The resounding blasts crashed from the mountaintop and filled the sky. Carter felt the wall shake. He clung to the pitons and watched as fiery debris streaked past him and the guard, inches above their heads.

The blasts came in staccato bursts now as rockets from Billings's companion ships added their muscle to the strike leader's firepower.

Heavy booms came, and Carter knew that the thousand-pounders were finding their marks. The wall shook. Concussions came in waves, forcing Carter to hang on tight, making the guard swing and buck on his dangling rope.

The crashing cannonade of explosions seemed to go on forever. By Carter's watch, however, the bombs and rockets took only a minute and twenty-eight point six seconds to level the south wing of the villa and send the sleeping guards and technicians fleeing to the northern end of the walled compound.

The machine guns from the throbbing, swooping, churning choppers kept the guards at the fence at bay and also managed to avoid the dangerous minefield.

When the earth and the wall stopped shuddering from the last bomb blast, Nick Carter raised his head and looked at the scene of devastation.

As he'd predicted, men were dashing out of the center and north wings of the villa, spilling into the open yard toward the northern wall. One of the choppers was pouring a withering fire into the gang of panicked, half-asleep men.

Carter picked up the Weatherby Mark V, chose a spot near the door of the guard shanty, and waited for the first men to reach it. A gang of perhaps twenty of them met at the door, pushing and shoving to get inside to the weapons there. Carter waited.

When the guards began to rush back out of the guard

shanty with the AK-47 rifles that Carter had disarmed, he opened up with the Weatherby.

It was as if the bombing had begun again. In the relative calm of the mountaintop, the Weatherby's throaty voice outdid the roar and throb of the helicopters swooping around like hungry eagles just above. Two men fell, and Carter squeezed off several more rounds, taking his time.

A group of six spotted his position from the tongues of flame and ran his way, aiming the empty AK-47s. Carter watched the surprised looks on their faces when they pulled their triggers and nothing happened. He took careful aim and shot all six.

A second group emerged from the shanty at the same time, running smack into a hail of steel and copper from one of the copters. Carter watched the rhythmic annihilation, saw a man cut in two by stuttering machine gun fire, saw the entire group drop to the ground dead or in agony.

Carter waited, letting the choppers do the work for now. His job, he knew, was to make certain no stragglers escaped. Before leaving the mountaintop, he also had to make certain the laboratories were destroyed and that no more nuclear bombs could be built there.

A survivor, angry and armed, could make that job difficult. He could kill Carter and make the job impossible.

Billings's chopper was at the southern end, finishing off the guards at the fence. The other choppers swooped back and forth, raking the villa and the northern wall with their big 50-calibers.

In six minutes and twelve point six seconds, the firing stopped. The three choppers began to circle the compound, watching. Carter eased to the top of the wall and stared into the darkness of the yard.

There was no activity at the northern end. All the guards and technicians who had gone that way were either dead or playing possum. It was also quiet at the fence. Not even the dogs were barking.

Carter was just raising the Weatherby to survey the villa with the sniperscope, when two AK-47 automatic rifles opened fire from a dark window. Carter felt and heard the hammerblows of the cuprosteel bullets that crashed into the wall inches from his head. He eased back over the side and took up his position on the pitons. He was just preparing to call Billings to order a rocket hit on that window when he noticed that something was wrong.

He was hanging by his secondary lifeline, not the nylon rope he had tied to the tree. Something else was missing.

The guard Carter had so carefully placed out of danger was gone.

Carter looked up and saw the frayed part of the white nylon rope. He knew what had happened. When the two automatics had opened up, the bullets had hammered into the top of the wall. They had missed Carter, but they had chewed up the nylon ropes, severing the only lifeline of the young guard Carter had wanted to save. Of all the killing going on tonight, that death affected him the most.

But there was no time to mourn. The vicious fire was still coming. And Carter's own lifeline went flying away from him, leaving him at the mercy of the four hastily set pitons.

At the same time the bullets severed his lifeline and forced him to grab hold of the two upper pitons, his radio slipped from his hand and went flying off into the darkness below.

He couldn't contact the helicopters for help in eliminating this latest threat to his life, to all his plans.

NINETEEN

Josh Billings was leading the merry-go-round check of the villa. He'd just passed the eastern wall and was heeling to port for a northerly sweep when he saw something fall from near the top of the wall and plunge into the jungle below.

That "something" hanging there beside Nick Carter had puzzled him from the moment the attack force had arrived to blast the laboratories and rake the compound with the chattering fifties.

When Billings had seen Carter crawl to the top of the wall, he'd hovered his craft, watching the dark villa and compound. He'd seen the twin blasts of firing from the villa window and noticed the thing beside Carter fall into the jungle.

And he knew. Carter had found someone—a friendly—or he'd taken a captive. And now the government agent was pinned down by a killing fire.

Billings checked his weapons. He had no rockets left. He'd dropped all his fire bombs. But the starboard 50-caliber and the nose-mounted 20mm were still armed and ready. He decided on the 20mm.

"A-Force Three, A-Force Two," he said into the

microphone. "All eyes on look-see for stragglers. Renegades in the window are mine."

He revved the engines, felt the biting torque of the swirling blades, and eased the big Bell Cobra into a neat dive. He came in low, virtually on a collision course with Carter who was clinging to the side of the wall, near the top.

Fifty yards shy of the wall, he raised the chopper, topped the wall by mere inches, and squeezed the red button on the cyclic pitch stick.

The chopper seemed to buck and stand still in the air as the 20mm shell burst from the cannon mounted in the nose. The pilot's eyes trailed the whizzing shell, and he waited for the telltale ball of fire to burst from the offending window before going into a power climb high over the villa.

By the time he'd circled back, Carter was walking across the compound toward the burning villa.

He gave the man from Washington five minutes to ascertain that the job had been done right, then he hovered over the agreed parallel and lowered the hook and cable.

Carter dashed from a dark doorway of the villa and leaped aboard the hook. Billings started the winch motor and brought the black figure into the flagship.

In less than a minute, Carter was in the copilot's seat and the three choppers were screaming toward the bivouac area.

The laboratories had been destroyed. There were no survivors on the mountaintop. There was no leaking radiation. It had been a perfect strike from a logistical standpoint. But Nick Carter seemed defeated, subdued.

"Who was the guy?" Billings asked as he took a 260° bearing for the bivouac area. "The guy who fell?"

"I never got his name," Carter said, his voice low. "He was just a kid. Brainwashed. I could have turned him around."

"You can't save 'em all."

"I can damned well try," Carter said, staring at the pilot.

"Yeah, I guess you can do that. What next? You got any ideas on how we hit that downtown building?"

Carter gazed out into the darkness. The silence, except for the hypnotic throbbing of the engine and flailing of the blades, was almost deafening.

"I have an idea," he said. "It involves putting the lives of good people on the line."

"I guess it always does."

"I'm going to use Irena," he told Billings. "I'm going to use her and probably get her killed. Also myself. Also a lot of people in San Juan."

Carter pressed his heavy shoulders into the seat back. He flashed a quick grin at the pilot, then stared glumly at the moonlit jungle below.

"That boy's death hit you hard," Billings said.

"There were a lot of boys up there. And a fine woman near Trujillo Alto."

"Sure," Billings said in a low, soft voice. "It's eulogy time, right?"

"No, just time for human compassion," Carter said, arching an eyebrow at the pilot.

And, Carter thought as he gazed at clouds scudding past a fast-dropping moon, *maybe time to finish the job*.

"I never thought soldiers took time out for compassion in the middle of a war," Josh Billings said.

Carter looked at him. "So now you're an expert on war?"

The captain grinned and shook his head. "No expert, sir, but I do believe I've learned a bit about it in the past twenty-four hours."

"I suppose you have. When it gets right down to it, war is a simple thing of killing or being killed. But right now, Captain Joshua Billings, newly ordained warrior, let's get this crate moving. We have to put the lives of some good people on the line."

Billings twisted the throttle to its highest notch, smiled at the man from Washington, and listened to the ear-splitting roar of the engine. Carter watched the night and thought of Irena, of his doubts about her. There was nothing to do but use her, and use her ruthlessly.

He watched her eyes as he told her the plan, reading them for truth or treachery.

Irena gazed back at him, listening to his words, absorbing what he said. Fear shone in her eyes. Was it fear of him and what he would do to the cause of Los Bravos, or was it fear that the dangerous plan wouldn't work, that the bomb would go off while they were in the building?

Carter frankly couldn't tell which way Irena's sentiments lay. But it didn't matter anymore. He'd use her either way. He thought he saw a look of compassion when he said that the plan required him to reopen the wound on his side.

"My God, Nick, is it necessary to go that far?"

They were sitting in his tent, listening to the soft wind of dawn whistle across the mountain outside. Carter was in a canvas folding chair beside the map table. Irena was on the cot. The kerosene lamp sizzled and spat, battling the daylight that would soon end its usefulness.

"It's necessary," he said. "If you're to convince Jorge Menalos that you've captured the man who has been creating havoc with his plans, you've got to bring me in wounded and helpless. Presumably helpless, anyway."

The plan was for Irena to telephone Menalos from a boat basin across the harbor from San Juan, and tell him how the man from Washington had "murdered" Antonio Vortez and how she had saved her own life by pretending to go along with the madman until her chance came.

The beautiful colonel was to say that she'd been secretly on the side of Los Bravos all along, and then she was to describe how she'd shot the man from Washington as they rode toward San Juan only hours before. She was to say that the special attack force had returned to Washington after destroying Alto Segundo.

Carter had given Irena several aces to play in case Menalos balked at having her bring the wounded agent to him. She was to reveal that Tranquilo had double-crossed him by having the bomb set to go off at ten that morning and not at eleven on Thursday. And she was to tell Menalos that the man from Washington knew how to reset the bomb.

"Do you?" Irena asked.

"No. There isn't any way to reset it. The thing either blows or Menalos can abort. If he aborts, there's a step-down procedure that takes several days."

"Won't he know this? After all, he is a nuclear physicist."

"He'll know it," Carter said, "but he's not a bomb expert. New things are being learned and developed every day. You're to tell him that I've been trained in the newest techniques at Los Alamos—that I can reset the bomb in his building."

"Can you?"

"It's immaterial. If Menalos thinks so, it will give him hope that his plan can still be carried out. Without hope, why would he care that you caught the rascal from Washington?"

"But," Irena said, twisting her fingers nervously and peering at Carter in the lantern light, "we will be inside that building. If the bomb goes off while we're there . . ."

"I know. We'll disintegrate, vaporize. The trick, Irena, is to get in, stop Menalos, abort the triggering device, and failing all that, get the hell out long before the bomb goes off."

"Yes." It was a very small yes.

"Will you do it?" Carter demanded.

"It's—it's just so risky. What makes you think that his guards will let me keep your gun once we're inside?"

"They will," Carter said. "Just keep it trained on me and act like an officer. At the right moment, when I give the signal, you flip the Luger to me."

Still she hesitated. "It's really dangerous, Nick. Isn't there a better way? I mean, I'm not scared for myself. But if that bomb goes off, thousands of my people will be, as you said, disintegrated. I guess I was hoping you'd come up with something really sure."

"Like the Sixth Fleet or the whole U.S. Army?"

"I suppose—something like that."

Carter laughed. "Have you forgotten Humpty Dumpty?" he asked.

"What does that have to do with this?"

"Everything, except he hasn't fallen off the wall yet. But all the king's horses and all the king's men—and all the armies in the world—can't undo what's been done in that building in downtown San Juan. In fact, the greater the numbers and the larger the force, the more likely it is that the bomb will go off on schedule. Right now, I'm all San Juan has—and you're all I have."

"So many things could go wrong," she said.

"Nothing will," Carter assured her.

She still looked worried. "I hope not. I sincerely hope not."

"Does that mean you'll go along with my silly plan?"

She sighed deeply and gazed out at the dawning light from the eastern mountains.

"For better or for worse, I'll go along with it. Heaven help us."

Carter grinned and took the lady into his arms. As he hugged her, he stared at the flickering, spidery light on the wall of the tent and wondered if he should tell her all the plan, tell her what he'd arranged with Billings and the attack force.

No, he decided. If things went wrong inside that building, it was best that she didn't know. She might panic.

For better or for worse, he thought bitterly, recalling

her words, *we'd damned well better make it work*. There was no slack cut for this job. None whatsoever.

At 7:30, after a short nap, Carter moved outside the command tent and stood on the mountaintop alone. He checked his weaponry beneath the neat sports outfit one of Captain Billings's men had retrieved from his apartment in the Old City. Wilhelmina was snug in her holster, Hugo was serene and cool against his arm, and Pierre—the last of the two gas bombs he'd brought on this mission—rode comfortably alongside his testicles. Carter's well-muscled frame still bore the marks of fatigue and weariness, but the nap had done wonders for him. He just might, he thought wryly, make it through the morning.

Irena emerged from her tent. She wore a simple shift that Billings's man had brought back when he'd gone after Carter's slacks and sport shirt. There was no sign of her wound, and he wondered if she'd taken off the dressing prematurely.

"Ready?" he asked.

She nodded and walked across the dew-damp ground and took his hand. They walked to the waiting Bell Cobra, nodded to Captain Josh Billings, and climbed aboard.

The next hour seemed to go swiftly. With Billings's help, Carter stole the necessary boat after the chopper put down in a meadow near the town of Catano, across the bay from the peninsula city. And then the three returned to the marina office, and Irena made the call.

The hard part was getting through the buffer of lieutenants Menalos had established to protect himself. But mention of Tranquilo and of the man from Washington opened ears. Shortly before nine o'clock, Irena had the nuclear physicist on the line.

She was convincing. She told it straight, just as Carter had given it to her. She was across the bay at Catano. She had a boat. The man from Washington was on the boat, wounded and unconscious.

She could bring the man to him, she told Menalos, but she needed help.

"Why should you bring him to me at all?" Menalos demanded. Carter, his ear close to Irena's, could hear the snarling voice clearly. "What are you trying to do, Colonel Balleta? I don't understand any of this about Tranquilo and a man from Washington."

Carter nodded. The authorities, Irena told Menalos, knew all about the bomb and how it had been set by Tranquilo's agent—the helicopter pilot—to go off in an hour, not on Thursday. Menalos stopped her.

"You're insane!" he screamed through the telephone. "I checked the triggering device myself!"

"The device you checked is a phony," Irena said, using Carter's well-coached words. "The real one is set to go off in"—she looked at her watch—"just fifty-eight minutes."

The line was silent as Menalos digested the shattering revelation. Carter nodded again, and Irena filled the silence:

"The man from Washington," she said, "knows how to reset the bomb without aborting, without a step-down time." She went on and on with technical details, talking rapidly, knowing that Menalos understood even if she didn't. He broke in on her again.

"Leave immediately!" he said. "My men will meet your boat. Hurry! There is no time to waste!"

Irena hung up and sagged in the phone booth. "It is done," she said as Carter's strong arms supported her.

"Yes, it's done. Let's get cracking."

Billings flew off in the Cobra, heading north across the ocean toward Miami. Carter and Irena watched as he joined the attack force and disappeared. Carter started the boat and showed Irena how to manipulate the throttle. As the boat churned out of the small cove into the immense harbor, Carter sat on a boat cushion and felt with his fingers the swollen welt of his side wound. He unleased

Hugo and used the stiletto to cut a jagged line in his clean
shirt. Irena turned once to watch, then kept her eyes dead
ahead as the man from Washington opened his healing
wound and let the blood flow freely onto his shirt and
jacket.

If nothing else, Carter thought as he watched his own
blood soak his clean clothing, *it sure as hell looks convincing.*

TWENTY

Nick Carter was exhausted. His thirty-five hours in Puerto Rico hadn't been blessed with any generous moments of tranquility. And the rocking boat was no comfort.

He lay on the cushions at the rear of the boat as it bumped the dock pilings. He saw the two men move up, then closed his eyes. He heard voices speak in rough, slang-filled street Spanish. Carter sensed more than saw Irena sitting beside him with Wilhelmina trained on his forehead.

"He is still unconscious," he heard her say. "Carry him gently. We don't want him to die before Señor Menalos talks to him."

Carter let himself go slack for the trip from the boat to the waiting car. As he lay on the floor of the back seat, he listened to the city's sounds, gauged distance and time, and felt more blood seep from his wound. He hoped he hadn't gone overboard with Hugo; half as much blood would have been just as convincing.

The car slowed after having stopped at a red light. Carter peered through slitted lids and saw a white building. Numbers came into view: 220.

They were there.

The car turned into an alley. Carter felt his heart pound harder, felt adrenaline pump through his veins. His body responded by pouring more blood through his wound, soaking his clothing and the floor of the car.

"*Madre de Dios*," one of his escorts snarled. "The pig has ruined my car."

"Don't worry," Irena responded. "Señor Menalos will buy you a new one."

The two men laughed, and hauled Carter's passive body from the rear seat and across a small parking area. Carter sneaked another peek, saw that he was being taken through a rear door, and closed his eyes again.

"Take him directly to Señor Menalos's office," Irena commanded. "He is to be questioned there."

"If he's still alive," one of the men countered.

"He'd better be alive," Irena snapped, a threatening tone to her voice. "Handle him more gently."

Carter felt a rush of pride for the beautiful officer. She was playing her part well. There was even a new brand of toughness in her voice, as though the part suited her.

The men stopped in a well-lighted corridor. Carter heard a door open, smelled cigar smoke from the room behind that door, then heard a smooth, oily voice.

"Welcome, welcome, welcome," the voice oozed. "Come in. Put him on the couch. There. There. Ah, you did well, Irena. That will be all, gentlemen."

Carter heard the door close and sensed that the men were gone. He wanted to look at the man with the unctuous voice, but he didn't dare. He was so close to either victory or unthinkable defeat. The silence lengthened.

Carter felt the old unease tighten his chest. His sense of danger heightened. Something was wrong. He fluttered one lid and peered through the lashes.

The beautiful colonel and the physicist-politician-terrorist who would turn San Juan into an inferno were embracing.

The embrace should have been his opportunity to

move. But Irena was watching him over Jorge Menalos's shoulder, and she was pointing Wilhelmina directly at his head.

"We know you're awake, Mr. Carter," Menalos said, cracking the stillness. "It's time for you to fulfill your promise and tell me the things I need to know."

Menalos turned. He was a smallish, handsome man with a thick black mustache. His eyes, black as coal, were on Carter. A smile touched the corners of his wide mouth. He wore a gray business suit, looking every bit the owner of an export-import firm, every bit a leader and not a nuclear physicist.

Yet he was a nuclear physicist, a brilliant one with a diabolical plan. Carter sat up and listened to that plan.

"It's very simple, Mr. Carter," Menalos told him from his chair behind an enormous mahogany desk. Irena sat on a chair beside the desk and held the Luger on Carter. "Irena and I have been in love since the first time that Tranquilo—that is to say, Colonel Emilio Sangre— arranged to have her deliver papers to me. She was also the colonel's unwilling lover. She turned to me because she detested that pig."

"From one pig to another," Carter said, looking at Irena. "Right, Colonel Balleta?"

Irena said nothing. Menalos grinned.

"Have your fun by calling names," the physicist said. "You have so little time for it. But let me finish. The colonel, for all his brilliance, was hopelessly in love with Irena. In time, he would have taken over Puerto Rico and would have become Irena's pawn. As such, my pawn. You see, I talked Irena into remaining with the colonel to keep in his good graces. To learn his plans."

Menalos paused, crushed out his cigar, and leaned forward. "Unfortunately, the colonel decided to keep her in ignorance. It wasn't until you came along that we began to learn things. Ultimately, my beloved Irena learned the most important part of the colonel's plan. It was she who brought you to me, Mr. Carter, not you who used her to get to me. You have outwitted yourself. She was very good, both with the colonel and with you. She was perfect.''

Carter could believe that. The woman was good, very good. She'd had him fooled. Almost.

"You really must admire her skills," Menalos boasted as he lit up another huge cigar. "She led you into that trap sprung by her half brother, Antonio Vortez. She even carried a special transmitter so that he could follow you. And she found and threw away the radio that you carried. Of course, getting shot was not a part of her plan, but things worked out. You killed the half brother she has always hated. You helped her to heal. She killed the colonel when he was about to reveal the location of my headquarters. And she let you lead yourself to me. You really have to admire such cleverness."

"Sure. I really admire her cleverness."

Menalos and Irena laughed. Menalos came around the desk. "You have served me well, Mr. Carter," he said, grinning. "I have done some swift planning since you revealed through Irena that the bomb is to go off at ten—just twenty minutes from now. For one thing, I will let the bomb explode as the treacherous Colonel Sangre planned. But Irena and I will survive, and she will become the general's aide. My ultimate purposes will still be served."

"You're forgetting one thing," Carter said. "Even if you left now, you couldn't get out of the blast area in time. Traffic is heavy in the city at this hour."

"Except by helicopter," Menalos said. "Ah, you thought I would kill the colonel's spy, the helicopter pilot who was trained to set the phony triggering device. Well, spies can be bought or persuaded, Mr. Carter. You of all people should know that. The man now waits on the roof to whisk Irena and me to safety. I would love to leave you to anticipate the moment the bomb explodes beneath your feet, Mr. Carter, but I cannot permit myself such a luxury. Irena, you will please shoot the man from Washington now.''

Nick Carter watched as Irena raised his Luger and pointed it at his head.

He smiled.

''There's one more thing,'' he said, sitting upright on the couch and rubbing his wound through the blood-soaked shirt. ''You really ought to know the one last arrangement I made.''

''Wait,'' Menalos said, gesturing for Irena to lower the gun.

''Don't trust him, Jorge,'' Irena snapped, jamming the big Luger toward Carter. ''He's very clever. Don't trust him.''

Menalos looked at his watch. ''We can give him two minutes. We have ample time. Perhaps what he has to say will be of value.''

''It will,'' Carter said. ''It may save your lives.''

Menalos smiled, but there was no delight in his eyes. ''Then by all means,'' he said, putting his arm around Irena, ''tell us of the final arrangement you have made.''

''For one thing,'' Carter said, ''my special attack force didn't go back to the States. Three helicopters are already circling this building. The pilots have orders to shoot down your helicopter unless I contact them by radio and tell them that I am aboard that copter.''

Menalos pulled away from Irena and faced her with an angry scowl.

''You told me nothing of this!''

''He is lying, Jorge! I saw the three helicopters disappear to the northwest, heading for the United States.''

''You saw them heading *toward* the States,'' Carter said, sliding his hand into the hole in his shirt. ''You didn't see them return.''

''What other surprises do you have for us, Mr. Carter?'' Menalos demanded.

"For starters," Carter said, "you don't have the twenty minutes you think you have. The three choppers will bomb this building to rubble at exactly nine-fifty, ten minutes from now."

Menalos glowered at him, looked at his watch, then stared at Irena. Her hand on the Luger was beginning to shake.

"I don't believe you," Menalos rasped. "Shoot him, Irena!"

Carter grinned, then looked directly into Irena's lovely eyes. "You made one big mistake," he said to her. "I would have trusted you all the way but for that mistake. You told me the first time we met that your father died when you were six and that your mother remarried. Later, you told me that both parents died and that Maria Escobar brought you up. In all that's happened here, that may seem a small point to remember, but I did remember it. For that reason, I took all the cartridges out of the gun you're holding."

Jorge Menalos, seeing his fine planning going down the drain, leaped at Carter, arms and legs flailing. Carter pulled his hand from his shirt and brought up the pencil-thin stiletto. It caught the would-be dictator in the throat. Blood spurted. Menalos dropped to the floor.

Irena screamed, aimed the Luger at Carter, and squeezed a dead trigger. Carter moved swiftly, brought the stiletto's hilt down on her head, and felt metal slapping bone. He saw Irena's eyes go dull, then close.

The beautiful woman hit the floor beside her lover, silent as death. But she wasn't dead. If there was time after he'd disarmed the bomb, Carter thought, he'd be back to get her. She was too beautiful and intelligent to kill, to let die. Surely there would be a way to turn her around, just as he'd hoped to turn that young guard's head around.

But time, Carter knew, was running out fast.

In precisely nine minutes, the three choppers would strike. The idea of a strike ten minutes before the bomb was due to go off represented a faint hope that by tumbling all that debris down on top of the atomic bomb, the blast would be minimized.

The main idea was for Carter to disarm the bomb and call off the strike. He could do that only if he had time to reach the helicopter on the roof and use its radio.

Carter knew, though, that he wouldn't have enough time to do all that. He had to get through Jorge Menalos's men and find the bomb. Carter loaded the Luger with a clip he had taped to his ankle.

The AXE Killmaster was ready.

He burst from the office with Wilhelmina in his right hand and Hugo in his left. The two men who had brought him up from the boat were the first in his sights, and he blew them away with the Luger. Behind them appeared four young followers of Los Bravos, frightened and unsure of themselves and their weapons.

Carter, hoarding his ammo against possible greater odds, dispatched two with well-aimed shots, then used the stiletto on the remaining two.

In the deathly silence of the fourth-floor corridor, he took out his tiny Geiger counter and heard a loud clicking.

He headed for the staircase. There were two men lurking near the top of it. He sent lead ahead, heard the great echoing booms, then screams, then silence. He went down.

On the third floor, he detected a slight lessening of activity from the Geiger counter. The clicks were still furious, but spaced farther apart.

Two more Los Bravos goons leaped from doorways. And two more died in those doorways from Hugo's blade. On the second floor, the Geiger counter faded. It was then that Carter knew where the bomb was.

Sprinting back upstairs, Carter snapped his eyes at his watch. Seven minutes.

On the third floor, more people were coming out of doorways, but they weren't part of Los Bravos. Carter recognized them by type. They were the Communist friends of Colonel Sangre. He snarled at them as he pounded by.

Irena was still on the floor, unconscious. Carter leaped over her and began to tear open drawers and cabinets. Nothing.

There were two doors in the back wall. One was open, revealing a bathroom. Carter tried the other. It was locked. He didn't dare shoot off the lock, although he was certain that Menalos had switched off the alarm apparatus that would trigger the bombs on interference. The physicist couldn't have gone to the roof if the mechanism hadn't been shut off. But a bullet in the wrong place could still set off the bomb.

Carter grasped the knob with both hands and snatched the closet door from its hinges.

And there it was, a huge bomb casing, taking up the bottom half of the closet. Carter strained to recall his briefing about atom bombs and the photos he'd been shown in Hawk's office.

He located the timing device but ignored it, knowing that it was a phony. He had to remove the front panel and get at the real timing device.

He checked the screws holding the panel in place. Phillips head. He'd seen a screwdriver when he'd been going through Jorge Menalos's desk drawers. He prayed that it was a Phillips head.

He was down to minus five minutes. And counting.

Knowing that death was inevitable no matter what he did next, Carter worked calmly and methodically. He got the screwdriver, removed the panel, and was studying the timing device attached between a metal bar and the bomb when he heard movement behind him.

"Leave it alone," the voice of Colonel Irena Balleta rang in his ears. "It is all over for us, but not for the people of my country. They will have their independence."

Carter turned and saw the woman with the Luger in her

hands. He realized he had left Wilhelmina on the desk.

In that moment, the sound of helicopter engines and rotors jarred their ears.

Billings and his three Bell Cobras were getting in place for the kill.

Four minutes and thirty seconds to strike time.

Irena looked toward the window but held the gun on Carter. She smiled.

"Their bombs and rockets won't stop the timer," she said. "The big one will still go off at ten as the colonel—"

She never got to finish. Carter had taken advantage of her weak moment, the one she'd used to look toward the window. He'd taken a flying leap, and his feet caught the woman in the chest.

Irena screamed. The pain, especially to her injured side, must have been excruciating. Carter felt no compassion. There was no time for compassion now. Three minutes and fifty seconds to strike time.

The chopper engines roared in the room. The Cobras were circling the building.

Colonel Irena Balleta fell against the big desk and let out another yell. Carter was on her. He snatched the Luger from her hands, caught her with a vicious uppercut, and sent her back to the land of Nod.

This time, there would be no further interruptions. With time running out, Carter placed Wilhelmina's muzzle against the beautiful blond head, swore, and squeezed the trigger.

At minus two minutes and forty seconds, he was back at the bomb, studying the triggering device.

The words of the briefing team members came back to him: *Don't touch the red wire; don't even graze it. The green wire is a dummy. Don't waste time on it. Look for the white wire. Remove it. If you don't have the proper tool, wrench the white wire loose with your bare hands.*

He couldn't see a white wire.

Carter sweated and looked. His vision blurred from the

intense concentration. He finally saw the white wire.

It was behind the red and green wires, in the narrow space between the bomb and the steel bar. He couldn't wrench it loose, even with the screwdriver, without touching the red wire. He looked at his watch.

One minute and two seconds left.

The roar of the Bell Cobras filled the room and all of Nick Carter's being. He'd come so far, done so much, endured both physical and emotional pain, only to run out of time and into an impossible situation.

There was no way to release that white wire and stop it from sending its electrical charge from the batteries in the timer to the TNT lodes that waited to slam into the subcritical mass of Pu-239. No way except one.

At precisely minus forty-two seconds, Carter aimed Wilhelmina at the wire, took care to make certain the bullet stayed in the open space, and fired.

The white wire blew away. Copper strands glinted back at Carter. The bomb had been disarmed. There would be no holocaust.

Except for Nick Carter.

No. He wouldn't accept that. There was still some time. Exactly thirty seconds.

Carter bolted for the door and ripped it open. He pounded down the stairs and was confronted by the whole group of Russians who had come from Cuba on the trawler. They were out in the hall, armed now, concerned about the helicopters.

"Nothing to worry about," he yelled in Russian. "You might as well go back to your—"

His words were interrupted by the crashing sound of a rocket that had apparently been fired prematurely through an upstairs window. The Russians nearly went berserk and began shooting pistols into the ceiling of the corridor. Carter took Pierre from his pouch, activated the little bomb, rolled him into the crowd of confused and frightened Russians, and plunged down yet another staircase.

As he came out onto the sidewalk, he heard the big bombs hitting the roof above and saw bits of debris shooting up in a cloud around the building at 220 Avenida Caliente.

It would all be destroyed. A disarmed and quite harmless atomic bomb. The man who would have ruled Puerto Rico with an iron hand. Twenty Russians who hoped to share in the newly cut pie. A beautiful woman who, in the end, could not be trusted.

Carter ran into the street, where cars were already coming to a halt and people—many of them tourists—were gawking up at the unmarked helicopters attacking an office building. As bits of fiery debris began to fall to the street, the people began to scream and to run helter-skelter.

Carter paused on the sidewalk across the street and watched the scene as the premises of San Juan Exports were ravaged by modern implements of war. The people below were in a panic now; there would be much official explaining of this mess to the people of Puerto Rico, but Carter was certain that the government could handle it.

For one thing, the people who were screaming right now would have been vaporized by an atomic explosion if that very government hadn't seen fit to have an organization like AXE and agents like Nick Carter. There would be few left to complain of fear and fiery debris—and a momentary halt to traffic.

Carter was about to turn away, to get to his apartment and report to Hawk and then catch up on some much needed sleep, when he heard something clatter to the pavement in the middle of the street. He turned and saw what it was—and so did several others who were peering at the curious object as though it were something dropped from Mars.

He grinned and looked up at the lead helicopter. The homely pilot had put the finishing touch on the strike, making it all a bit easier on the government.

The object that had fallen to the street was a shiny, decorative machete, a token of a strike by the terrorist organization known as Los Bravos.

"Nice touch, Josh," Carter said aloud as he turned once again and walked away from the ruined, smoking building, and from the departing helicopters. "You'll make a fine warrior someday."

DON'T MISS THE NEXT NEW NICK CARTER SPY THRILLER

CIRCLE OF SCORPIONS

Behind him, the footsteps slowed in caution. They thought they had the Killmaster boxed, and now, hopefully, they would move in for the kill.

Carter darted through the opening and left the heavy door open a crack behind him.

It was a large wine cellar, fitted with long rows of racks on which rested many hundreds of dusty bottles under a white-washed stone roof. He darted along the wall, glancing hurriedly down each row. Each ended in a blank stone wall . . . except the last. At the far end of that was a small vaulted door.

Nick checked it, and smiled in satisfaction when he found it locked.

There was no other way out.

Now, the Killmaster thought, settling into a crouch behind one of the high wine racks, the hunted becomes the hunter.

A tenseness in the muscle of his right forearm released

the spring in Hugo's sheath, sending the deadly stiletto sliding forward into his hand.

There was a deathly silence, and then the faint creak of the entrance door opening. Without hesitation, Carter clutched a half-bottle of wine from one of the racks and threw it unerringly at the bulb.

There was a popping sound as the light went, and then a louder crash as the bottle shattered on the stone floor. This was quickly followed by guttural curses and the sound of falling bodies as the two of them rolled into the room. Then Carter heard the dull thud of the door closing behind them.

He's not armed, the squat man had said after patting Nick down.

Hopefully, he had relayed this information to the two outside men and the woman.

Now the cellar was completely dark. Clutching the stiletto in his hand, Carter crouched in a corner and reasoned his next move. There were two of them, and shortly they might be joined by a third, the woman.

They would probably use knives, but Carter guessed they would have guns as well. He could only hope that they, like himself, wanted to keep this private. If so, guns wouldn't be a factor.

Since there were only two of them, they couldn't search the passages between the rows of wine racks one by one and be sure that he hadn't slipped by at the unguarded end.

Carter guessed that one would start by feeling his way carefully around the perimeter walls, either to drive him toward the other one who would be waiting for him, or to make Nick move and perhaps betray his whereabouts by some slight noise.

If Carter was guessing correctly, what was the best maneuver to counter it?

His only hope was to get at one of them first and hope the other would go for the sound in the confusion.

The problem was, which way to go? He didn't know

which way round the outer walls they would be moving.

Still crouching, he listened intently. There was no footfall, but then, if they were moving, it was probably on their hands and knees.

Then he thought he heard a faint clink, as though one bottle had been touched against another. It seemed to have come from the far end of the right-hand wall leading away from his corner.

Still in a half-crouch, his toes barely making a whisper on the stone floor, Nick moved to his right. As he came to the corner at the far end of the wall along which he was moving, he stopped to listen once more. He was sure that the wall he had now reached was the one that led to the entrance door.

He thought of making a noise and drawing them in, when he heard the breathing, almost beside him.

With the greatest care, the Killmaster groped for the end of the nearest wine rack and eased himself across the space and into the passage between that rack and the next. In spite of the exertion, he managed first to hold his breath, and then to breathe cautiously and silently.

What he could not decide was whether, a moment or two earlier, his own breathing had been as apparent to the man as his had been to Carter.

The breathing could no longer be heard. He dug in the pocket of his slacks until his fingers found a pack of matches. Carefully, he tucked the flap under the matches and folded two of them down. Holding the match heads in place with his thumb over the striking surface, he concentrated hard, trying to discern the slight indication of where his prey was.

And then he heard it; the barely perceptible scrape of a toe or the leather sole of a shoe against the stone. It came from the wall directly opposite him.

Tensing his whole body, Carter scraped the matches over the flint.

They had fooled him. One was directly in front of him,

staring at the flaring matches in Carter's left hand in surprise. But the other one wasn't across the room as Carter had thought. He was in the next aisle over, and already moving around toward him.

But now the Killmaster only had time for the one in front of him as the man lunged. Nick thrust forward with his left hand, smashing the burning matches into the man's face. His right hand, holding the stiletto, flashed up from the floor.

There was a scream of pain as the matches seared the man's face, but it became a dry rattle as the stiletto found a home in his throat. It was dark again, but Carter knew the man was done when he felt warm blood run across his hand.

Number one dropped like a stone and, just as he hit, the second one struck a clubbing blow across Carter's back. It sent Nick reeling against the wall. He hit, whirled, and swung his left arm.

It was a lucky blow. The heel of his hand struck number two full in the face. He could feel cartilage, bone and muscle all turn to gel. Then the man was sliding down his body, trying to hold on as Carter tried as hard to twist free.

Somehow, he managed to seize an ankle and pull. Carter's feet went out from under him, and as he went down the stiletto came out of his hand. He heard it hit the floor and slither off somewhere under the bottles. In an instant, the whole weight of the other man's body fell on Nick, knocking the breath from him and pinning him down.

Just as quickly, Carter felt himself being flipped. A hand slid across his face and the inner side of an elbow sought his throat.

The intent was all too clear. The man was going to bend Carter's head back until the spine snapped.

Nick tensed his throat muscles before the grip became stationary. At the same time, he managed to get his chin slightly under the man's wrist.

It wasn't much for leverage, but it was enough to sink his teeth deeply into the flesh.

He bit down with all the strength in his jaws, bringing a howl of pain from the man's throat. Carter waited until he could taste blood and feel bone with his teeth, and then he started grinding.

It worked.

The arm loosened from his throat. Nick bucked upward, raising the straddling body off of him. Before the man could come back down again, the Killmaster flipped over and brought both knees up in a crunching blow to the other's groin.

There was another howl of pain and he fell limply forward. Carter brought his left forearm across the windpipe, folded his right arm around the neck, and pressured it in a vise.

Even in unconsciousness the man struggled, but only for a few seconds. Then he settled down against Nick again.

Carter was about to push the very dead weight off him, when there was a scraping sound and a sudden shaft of light.

—From CIRCLE OF SCORPIONS
A New Nick Carter Spy Thriller
From Charter in January 1985

☐ 71539-7	RETREAT FOR DEATH	$2.50
☐ 79073-9	THE STRONTIUM CODE	$2.50
☐ 79077-1	THE SUICIDE SEAT	$2.25
☐ 82726-8	TURKISH BLOODBATH	$2.25
☐ 09157-1	CARIBBEAN COUP	$2.50
☐ 14220-6	DEATH ISLAND	$2.50
☐ 95935-0	ZERO-HOUR STRIKE FORCE	$2.50
☐ 03223-0	ASSIGNMENT: RIO	$2.50
☐ 13918-3	DAY OF THE MAHDI	$2.50
☐ 14222-2	DEATH HAND PLAY	$2.50
☐ 29782-X	THE GOLDEN BULL	$2.50
☐ 45520-4	THE KREMLIN KILL	$2.50
☐ 52276-9	THE MAYAN CONNECTION	$2.50

Prices may be slightly higher in Canada.

Available at your local bookstore or return this form to:

CHARTER BOOKS
Book Mailing Service
P.O. Box 690, Rockville Centre, NY 11571

Please send me the titles checked above. I enclose _____. Include 75¢ for postage and handling if one book is ordered; 25¢ per book for two or more not to exceed $1.75. California, Illinois, New York and Tennessee residents please add sales tax.

NAME _____

ADDRESS _____

CITY _____ STATE/ZIP _____

(allow six weeks for delivery.)   A8